THE

INFINITY

CAVERNS

STUART JAFFE

The Infinity Caverns is a work of fiction. Names, characters, places, and incidents either are the product of the author's imagination or are used fictitiously, and any resemblance to any persons, living or dead, business establishments, events, or locales is entirely coincidental.

THE INFINITY CAVERNS

Copyright © 2017 by Stuart Jaffe
Cover art by Deranged Doctor Design

ISBN 13: 978-1547270729
ISBN 10: 1547270721

First Edition: July, 2017
Second Edition: October, 2019

For Glory and Gabe,
of course

Also by Stuart Jaffe

Max Porter Paranormal Mysteries
Southern Bound   Southern Curses   Southern Fury
Southern Charm   Southern Rites   Southern Souls
Southern Belle   Southern Craft
Southern Gothic   Southern Spirit
Southern Haunts   Southern Flames

Nathan K Thrillers   *Parallel Society*
Immortal Killers   The Infinity Caverns
Killing Machine   Book on the Isle
The Cardinal   Rift Angel
Yukon Massacre   Lost Time
The First Battle
Immortal Darkness
A Spy for Eternity
Prisoner
Desert Takedown

The Malja Chronicles
The Way of the Black Beast
The Way of the Sword and Gun
The Way of the Brother Gods
The Way of the Blade
The Way of the Power
The Way of the Soul

Stand Alone Novels   *Gillian Boone Novels*
After The Crash   A Glimpse of Her Soul
Real Magic   Pathway to Spirit
Founders

Short Story Collection
10 Bits of My Brain   10 More Bits of My Brain
The Marshall Drummond Case Files: Cabinet 1
The Bluesman

Non-Fiction
How to Write Magical Words: A Writer's Companion

THE

INFINITY

CAVERNS

CHAPTER 1

Veronica Rider, "Roni" to her friends, unlocked the door to the *In The Bind* bookshop and entered with a tipsy giggle. It had been a long time since she went on a date and even longer since she had bothered to drink alcohol. Two glasses of Riesling had gone to her head.

The Old Gang sat at a large square table that dominated the center reading area of the store. Gram, Elliot, and Sully all raised their heads from the store's ledgers to smile at her. Roni thought of them as the Old Gang mostly because they had been running the store since before she had been born. But also, the youngest of the group, Elliot, had recently celebrated his sixty-seventh birthday.

"How'd the date go?" Gram asked. Lillian Donaugh, aka Gram, was a rotund woman who had owned *In The Bind* from age twenty-two. The business had been in Roni's family for five generations.

"Fine," she said.

Elliot laughed. He was a large, shiny-bald black man with a larger voice. Born in Kenya, he moved to England in his twenties and then to America at forty-two, and as a result, he spoke in an exact manner as if he feared being misunderstood. "Lillian, you cannot attack the kids with those kinds of questions. Roni does not want to discuss her sexual life with her grandmother."

"Who's talking sex?" Gram said. "I just wanted to know if the date went well."

Sully, a small man with white tufts of hair ringing his head, pushed his glasses up his nose as he looked up from the ledger. "Asking if a date *went well* is the same as asking if she ended up in bed."

Gram scoffed. "Oh, poo on that. You two are the dirtiest old men I know."

"We're the only old men you know. The rest are dead."

Elliot laughed again. "Roni, you must ignore your Gram. We are happy you had a good time. You deserve it after that unfortunate man you were dating. Bob? Billy?"

"Brian," Roni said. "Thanks."

"Bastard was more like it." Gram finished writing in a few numbers and closed the ledgers. "All done for tonight. Roni, hon, will you be a dear and put these back under the register?"

"You know, I've heard there's a new-fangled contraption called a computer. It could make all that bookkeeping a ton easier."

The Old Gang stood and stretched their weary bones. Sully had a slight stoop but he appeared to straighten a bit as he said, "Sometimes, the old ways are the best ways. Never forget the power of writing words to paper. It'll amaze you."

Elliot grabbed his cane, a gnarled oak limb that he had shellacked years ago. "Ignore these old fools. When you take over, you should go ahead and modernize this place."

Roni had no intention of letting the business go under, but she also had no intention of taking over. She wanted something different for her life. Though, at thirty-two, she had hoped to have figured out what that different thing was by now.

She stepped down to the sunken reading area and collected the ledgers. "Good night, everyone."

A quick round of hugs followed. Gram grabbed her big bag — an oversized purse that she never went without — and the Old Gang meandered toward the back. An elevator would take them to the fifth floor of the bookshop where they lived.

Roni took a moment to embrace the quiet of the store at night. With only a few dim lights on, the place closed in like a warm blanket. She had grown up here — played hide 'n' seek amongst the tall aisles of endless books, hurried over after school for a snack with Gram at the big, square table, had her first kiss in the Romance section, and her first breakup near the Mysteries. If she hadn't gone away to college, she probably would have lost her virginity in the Erotica section.

A knock at the door startled her. She peered out the window to find Darin, her date, waving like a fool. Perhaps it was his dimpled grin or the rich flock of dark hair on his head, or perhaps she had been taken in by his deep voice or the fact that she had not been out in the seven months since Brian had left — whatever the reason, she felt a satisfied warmth about Darin. She chuckled at his goofiness as she let him inside the store.

A shy voice in her head reminded her that she had only just met this man a few days ago. He had walked into the bookshop one morning, spent over an hour searching the aisles, and when he finally brought a few books to the counter to purchase, he asked Roni to dinner. The question took her so off-guard that she stammered a polite refusal.

But he flashed a friendly smile and said, "I understand. These days you can't be too careful. It's a shame, though, that a man can't ask a woman on a date anymore without having known her for several weeks first. I mean, the whole point of a date — well, an initial date anyway — is to get to know each other. Right? To see if there's any chemistry. I looked over at you from that aisle and I could feel my heart beating faster. I just had to try. I really want to know if the woman on the inside is as beautiful as the woman on the outside. I'm sorry. I hope I didn't embarrass you."

"Yes."

"I truly didn't mean to. I'll get out of here and —"

"I meant that yes, I'll go out with you."

If pressed, Roni would never be able to answer why she had changed her mind. She guessed it was a combination of thoughts and feelings mixed with the simple desire to break free from her mundane life. Being single and unemployed did not fill her with joy too often. Why not go on a date and be treated with some attention?

As Darin entered the bookshop that night, he inhaled deeply. "I love the smell of an old bookstore."

"I never notice it anymore." Roni flicked off the back row of lights. She didn't want Gram to find out she had brought somebody in after hours.

"Oh, that's a shame. That old paper, the glue, the dust — it all blends into this special aroma that you can only find in a place like this." He walked along the main aisle, his footsteps making dull thumps on the wood floor, and his fingers trailed along the stacks. "You said this place belongs to your grandmother?"

"That's right. I guess one day it'll belong to me."

"Won't it go to your parents first?"

Roni hesitated. Darin looked back and she could see the worry on his face. "It's okay," she said. "My mother died when I was little."

"I'm sorry."

"You didn't know. And that's the point of a first date, right? Getting to know each other."

He grinned, but it didn't ease her much. "The first date ended an hour ago. I really enjoyed it, and well, I couldn't wait for a second date. So, here I am."

She couldn't help the warmth that reddened her face. "Okay. Date number two."

"Okay, then. Tell me about your mother."

Roni leaned against the cash register. "Not much to tell. She was a wild one. She liked cars, men, and hard booze. One night, she went out and picked up all three. Ended up dead in a ditch with a steering wheel around her neck. My father couldn't handle it. I used to think it was the cheating that got him, but as I get older, I think he just loved her so much that he couldn't function in a world without her. But he's a religious man. Suicide was not an option for him. So, he buried himself in his Bible, and that's where he'll be until age takes its toll."

She had not intended to say so much, and thankfully, stopped before divulging the rest — especially that her father lived as an inpatient at Belmont Behavioral Hospital in West Philadelphia. The dark mood that followed her words threatened to destroy the start of their impromptu second date, but Darin must have sensed the same and quickly changed the tone. "You know," he said, "from the outside, I thought this place was going to be huge."

Hiding a sniffle, she said, "It is big. Five floors. But the top floor is broken up into two apartments — Gram's apartment and one for her two business partners. The third and fourth floors are for our highly collectibles — things we can't put on display for various reasons. Sometimes it's liability. Sometimes the books are so frail, they need to be in a specially-designed climate controlled area — which we had built on the fourth floor over a decade ago."

"And the second floor?"

"More books. There's a staircase in the back and an elevator off to the side. You want to go up there?"

"No need. I was just curious."

He watched her for a short time. He had done so several times over the course of their earlier dinner, and each time, she felt an odd mixture of emotions — her body flushed with warmth at the attention even as her skin crawled under the scrutiny. Maybe she had been stupid to agree to any of this. She had the sudden urge to be done with him — at least for the night — yet she didn't want to offend him by asking him to leave.

Instead of returning his deep gaze, she stepped behind the counter. "Oh, no. I forgot all about the day's records. Gram won't be happy when she sees I didn't update the ledgers. I was so excited about the date, I simply closed up without finishing the job."

"Go ahead and finish it up. I'll tell you about my parents while you work — if that won't be too much of a distraction," he said.

Unsure of how to make it any clearer that she was done for the night, and unsure of how he might take a more direct approach, she flashed a smile. "Sure. Okay," she said, and opened up her laptop. Tapping away on her computer, she pretended to finish up her work.

"My parents were decent folks." He rested his back against the end of one aisle. "I owe them a lot. They taught me to think for myself and to think critically — two things most kids don't learn anymore. My mother showered me with affection. A little smothering at times, but she always made sure I knew how proud she was of me. Above everything I could mention, though, the greatest gift they ever gave me was a love for reading. Going to the bookstore or the library or even getting to spend an hour browsing through Amazon — those were events for me. They wanted me to adore the written word, so they made sure each book I purchased, each book I read, each book I casually glanced at meant something."

"Sounds like good people."

"They were. My father worked in construction and my mother taught high school English. Not very high-brow professions but honest ones. They were the kind of people that never thought twice about helping out a neighbor. Real quality folks." He let his eyes wander around the bookstore. "It's because of them that I love places like this. I'm also rather fond of the people who work at places like this."

Roni forced herself to yawn. "That's sweet, but I'm really tired. I wasn't expecting a second date so soon, and I do have to work tomorrow."

"I thought you were unemployed."

"I am, but I work here a few times a week. I don't get paid, but I like to help out." She made a cheering motion with her fist. "Gotta get out there and find a job, too."

Darin paused, and Roni could not read the look on his face. She braced herself for any possibility. "Sure," he finally said, and headed toward the front door.

She wanted to smack herself. This poor guy clearly hadn't meant any harm, and now he would be leaving feeling rejected. And she liked him. Their dinner date had gone well.

"I'm sorry," she said, inwardly cringing at the meek sound of her voice. "I really don't mean to be rude. I told you at dinner that I haven't dated in a long time. This all feels a bit new."

"It's okay. You should never have to apologize for being truthful. You're tired and you've got to finish the bookkeeping. I understand."

Roni closed her laptop in case he saw that she had been

playing Candy Crush. "Maybe we can go out again another night."

"Sure." He put his hand on the door. "You want to know what I always loved most about a bookstore like this? It's the little hidden places. There's always some extra special room where the really cool stuff is kept. I mean, you mentioned the third and fourth floors, but I bet you've got a basement level, too. Right?"

Roni frowned. "We do. But it's mostly old magazines and stuff that needs to be sorted through."

He snapped his fingers. "That's what I'm talking about. That's the kind of space that thrilled me when I was a kid. You never knew what you were going to find down there." He lowered his chin and lifted his brow. "I don't suppose, maybe, you'd let me see it real quick. I promise I'll go after that. It's like a nostalgia thing for me."

"I don't know. It's late."

"Please?"

She figured she had already been rude enough. Plus, if she played along, she would be done with this faster. With as much levity as she could summon, she said, "Okay. But only five minutes. Then I've got to call it a night."

As she led the way, she could feel his eager energy like a hot lamp shining on her back. She walked down the stairs and flicked on the basement light. The large area had a low ceiling and a musty odor. Many of the boxes had been sitting around for years. An old dining room table had been placed underneath one of the four bare bulbs that lit the basement.

"That's where the magic happens," she said with a slight chuckle. "We sort through boxes and decide what stays and what goes."

Darin approached the table with a bit of reverence. A crate sat to the side with a crowbar resting nearby. Books had been piled in the crate. Stacks of old LIFE and TIME magazines formed miniature towers against the table legs. He stepped in close and brushed his fingertips along the top of the table. "I could spend hours down here. Just give me a good book and I'd sit here and read away the day. You're so lucky to have this place whenever you want it."

"I never really thought of it that way."

"You should. Books are too important to take for granted." His eyes lifted to a door on the wall opposite the table. A large padlock like something from a medieval dungeon prevented the door from opening. "What's that all about?"

"Gram's private collection. And before you even ask, the answer is *No*. Nobody gets to go in there. I mean it. I grew up in this bookstore and I've never even seen it."

He shrugged. "We all have our secrets. I guess your grandmother likes to have hers a little more clearly marked than most."

Roni flickered the lights. "Okay. Your five minutes is up. Time to go."

"It went fast, but I thank you."

Darin went back upstairs and stopped at the register. He reached out and took hold of Roni's hand. She let her hand hang limp but he clamped down tight.

"I guess this is good night again." He raised her hand to his lips. "A bit shorter than I had hoped for but a pleasant second date anyway."

"I suppose we should —"

He yanked her closely and pressed his mouth against hers. She pushed him back, pulling her hands free, and made two fists.

Raising his hands as his face dropped in shock, he said, "I'm so sorry. I thought you wanted me to kiss you."

"You need to go."

"I'm sorry. I don't know why —"

"Please, go now."

"I know. I'm so sorry. I'll go. Could you just — and I'm real sorry to ask — but could I have a glass of water or something? I feel faint. This isn't like me, and I think I'm panicking here."

She looked him over. He had broken out into a sweat and his skin looked pasty. "Stay here," she said and hurried to the side room that had a refrigerator, a sink, and some cupboards.

As she grabbed a coffee mug and filled it with water, she had to marvel at how strange the evening had become. Why did Darin have to go ruin everything? Their dinner had been light, fun, and friendly. Why the pressure for this crappy attempt at a second date romancing? If he only had shown some patience, she probably would have ended up sleeping with him. A normal second date a few nights later. And on the third, she would have been itching to take him. But now — there would not be another date. She didn't even want to see him again once he left the store.

When she returned with the mug of water, Darin was no longer at the register. The front door was locked, so he could not have left the building. Setting the mug on the counter, she walked up and down the main section of the floor, glancing across from aisle to aisle.

Her heart hammered in her chest. She knew a few self-defense moves from a class she took at the Havertown YMCA a few years ago, but her racing thoughts made it difficult to focus. When she reached the back of the store, her stomach twisted — the stairs. She knew it. He had gone down into the basement.

"Darin?" she called, but not too loudly.

No answer.

"Darin?"

A loud thump came from below.

She put a tentative foot on the top step. Another thump. But before she went further, her mind woke up — she had a small container of pepper spray in her purse. Hustling across the bookshop, she tried to ease the tightness in her chest. No good.

She rummaged through her purse but couldn't find it. At length, she upended the contents onto the counter. The pepper spray fell out last. Snatching it up, she rushed back to the stairs.

Listening intently, she tried to make out what he might be doing. A metal clang followed a wooden creak.

"Oh, crap," she whispered.

Despite the sense of urgency surrounding her, Roni could only manage to take one step every few seconds. The closer she came to the basement floor, the harder each step felt. Her legs thickened like cement, fighting her from moving forward.

In a desperate desire for normalcy to reassert itself, she wanted to call out again, to have Darin call back and assure her that all was fine. She wanted to step onto the floor and find him sitting at that table, thumbing through an old magazine. He would have a sheepish look and would profusely apologize. He would leave and all would be right once more.

Except none of that happened.

When she reached the bottom of the stairs, she found the lights on but no Darin. He did not sit at the table. He did not thumb through a magazine. He did not offer his apologies.

Instead, she saw what she feared she would see. The crowbar was missing, and the padlock to Gram's private room had been pried open. It lay in pieces on the floor.

The door stood ajar.

CHAPTER 2

Roni's teeth chattered together. Part of her wanted to race upstairs and ring for Gram. This was her room, after all. She should know that somebody had broken in. But another part of Roni feared what Gram might think.

Would she assume Roni had taken this man downstairs for a private fling? Of course, she would. Gram had many great qualities, but she also rushed to judgment, and her judgment could be harsh.

Once when she was eight, Roni wanted to help shelve the latest acquisitions. She didn't know one book from the other, so she picked up the first to catch her eye — a first edition of *Tropic of Cancer*. She never bothered to open the book, but merely started looking for a place to shelve it. When Gram saw her walking off with the book, she assumed her granddaughter wanted to read some dirty words. Gram snatched the book away and punished Roni with three weeks of cleaning the restrooms.

Standing at that open door in the basement, Roni wondered what Gram would do to her this time. After all, this room had been marked *off limits* all of Roni's life. But if she could get Darin out of there without disturbing anything, maybe Gram would never know.

In her quietest voice yet, Roni said, "Darin?"

No answer. Of course.

With small steps, she entered the room. At first, it appeared to be a bunker for books — a metal box of a room with metal shelves lined with numerous old leather-bound volumes. Fluorescent lights hung from the tiled ceiling.

As Roni walked deeper into the room, she noticed that the air grew colder with each step. The only sound — the tentative click of her heels. She stopped twice to listen for Darin but heard nothing. When she reached the back end of the room, she understood why.

A large hole in the wall opened into a cavern. A cavern? But that was the only word for it that Roni could think of. Stone walls carved out by millions of years of underground rivers and lakes. Dirt and rock stubbled the uneven ground. Stalactites hung from the ceiling, and a twisty path led downward and away.

Cool air wafted over her as she gazed out with her mouth agape. The steady trickle of water echoed off the curving walls. And in the walls, somebody had wired lights and carved bookshelves.

But as Roni followed the maze of turns further into the cavern, she noticed that the books were even stranger than their location. They were all extremely old, hardbacked, many bound in leather and a few in metal. For a while, none of them had titles — merely colored diamond shapes as if that were information enough. However, after a few minutes of walking, she came upon a new section of books unlike the others.

The cavern walls had narrowed to the width of a typical library aisle. On one side, she saw books with strange symbols on the spines and covers. Not occult symbols or

New Age symbols or anything she had encountered before. Rather, these looked like symbols of a unfamiliar language, like Tolkien's elvish, one created by a single mind and not a system evolved over centuries of a civilization. On the other side, she saw similar books, except these had chains attached to the spines that stretched to rings embedded into the stone walls as if the books were held prisoner with no hope of escape.

Roni's curiosity could not stop her churning stomach. Coupling Gram's desire to keep this place secret with the chained books spelled danger in bold red letters. Roni backed up several steps. She should hurry up to Gram's apartment, wake the old lady, and get her down here. Gram would know the fastest way to find Darin and she would know which books to stay away from.

Before Roni could head up toward the bookshop, however, a loud *whoosh* came from further below followed by the unmistakable sound of a man groaning.

"Darin?" she called out. No response. "Darin, let me know you're okay. I'm not mad at you. I just want to make sure you aren't hurt."

The groan returned — drawn out and muddy.

She hastened her pace downward. Gram would have to wait. Darin's groans suggested he had fallen and needed help. Plus — and Roni felt a twinge of guilt for this thought — there was still the possibility of finding Darin and getting him out of the basement before Gram ever found out.

As she rounded a wide bend, she saw tall stone pillars reaching into the darkness of the high ceiling. Books spiraled up along the pillars, some so high nobody could ever reach them without a fireman's ladder or sturdy scaffolding. Other books were higher still.

The groans continued and their echoes brought back a

ghostly sound. She continued on, the periodic sconces her only light source. As the ground leveled out, she came upon a door nestled into the stone. It stood open.

She entered a reading room with two long tables for research and study as well as four overstuffed chairs for more casual reading. Next to each chair stood a tall reading lamp and two smaller desk lamps provided light for those at the tables. Darin sat at the furthest table, a thick volume placed right in front of him.

"Darin? Are you okay?"

With his eyes closed, he said, "Better than okay. After all the searching, after the countless times I doubted this place even existed, I'm finally here."

"I don't understand what any of this is, but we need to go back upstairs."

"Let me show you."

He lifted the cover of the book before him and it slammed out of his hands and flattened, fully open, on the table. A bright blue light burst from the pages. The whooshing sound from earlier filled the room. As if a door on a jet plane opened at twenty thousand feet, the room depressurized and the book sucked everything towards it.

The big chairs slid towards the book. The desk lamps sparked as the cords wrenched free from their power source and then tumbled into the book. Straight into the pages — through them — as if the book was a deep pit.

Roni stumbled forward a few steps. The wind grew stronger. She leaned away, reaching for the door as if caught in a sudden squall.

Darin's satisfied smile dropped into horror. He gripped the edge of the table and leaned away from the open vacuum of the book.

Roni clung to the door jamb. She yelped as her legs lifted off the ground. She heard Darin scream and his head went in first. As his shoulders sunk into the pages, his white knuckled hands kept their lock on the table — the only thing saving him.

With Darin's body blocking much of the book, Roni's legs settled onto the floor. The wind was still strong, but she could stand on her own. Part of her screamed to run, get safe, and ignore everything else. But she searched for some way to help Darin. Except if she moved in close to that book and freed him, the hurricane would resume and she would be swept into those pages.

Maybe she could use a rock to dislodge the cover and force it closed. The idea seemed far-fetched, but nothing else came to mind. Tears welled in her eyes. If he died, she would be partly to blame. Straining towards the door, she tried to recall what rocks she had seen on her walk to this bizarre room.

Everything changed when she reached the door — Gram, Elliot, and Sully stood in the way.

"Gram, I'm so sorry," Roni cried out, but Gram did not pay her any attention. The old woman's eyes locked onto Darin.

She stepped forward and opened one hand. A long chain dropped loose from her sleeve. As she twirled the chain at her side, Sully scooted over to Roni.

He pushed her towards the wall and pressed an arm on either side of her. "It'll be okay," he said and lowered his head as if he tried to move the wall.

Looking over his shoulder, Roni watched as Gram whipped the chain across the room. It latched onto the spine of the book like a giant magnet. Jerking the chain, she pulled it clear off the table, leaving Darin behind. The massive winds returned.

Roni fell forward and would have toppled over into the book if not for Sully blocking the way. He remained motionless like a stone statue, his feet firmly planted in the floor. Gram did not slide toward the open pages either. Instead, she leaned back as if in a tug-o-war with the book. Elliot held onto the chain with one hand and his cane with the other. He wore a tall-collared cape that fluttered and snapped in the harsh winds.

Darin did not fare so well. He shrieked as his grip on the table's edge slipped. The howling air continued to pull him in. Tears streamed out of his eyes and into the book, never getting the chance to touch his cheeks.

Yelling above the cacophony of wind, Elliot said, "Hold on, young man! Do not give up!"

With stuttering steps, Elliot worked his way along the chain. Once he reached as close as he dared, he locked his arm around the chain and with his free arm, he stretched toward the book with his cane. The end of the cane bumped the cover. Elliot tried to work the cane underneath to close the book, but he needed to get closer.

"Forget it," Gram yelled, the strain in her voice matching that of her entire body as she leaned further back. "Get the boy."

Elliot shifted his body toward Darin. He pressed his feet into the floor and reached out with the cane. "Grab hold," he said.

Darin stared at the cane, a lifeline dangling before him. But Roni could see the way his arms trembled. To reach for the cane meant letting go. If he missed ...

"You can do it," Elliot said.

Darin shook his head and buried his face into the table.

"Come on, now. Grab the cane."

Roni shouted, "Darin, do it!"

He gazed up at her. His eyes glistened. Everything she saw in his face screamed of his doubt. Even before he made his half-hearted attempt, she knew he had given up.

Fumbling his hands free, he flapped his arms about, bumped the cane, but had no control.

Elliot lunged along the chain. But when he reached the book, Darin had already fallen in. Elliot had only time enough to pry his cane beneath the book and slam the cover closed. Any longer, and he would have joined Darin.

The wind died instantly. Sully straightened, as much as he could, and placed his hands on Roni's shoulders. "All over now."

Gram rushed forward. She stepped by Elliot without any notice of him and grabbed the book. With furious energy, she wrapped the chain around the book seven times before tucking the end underneath. Only then did she look at the others.

"Everybody okay?"

Elliot said, "I think so. Though my arthritis is going to flare up in the morning."

"You think you've got it bad? You can take a pill for your pain," Sully said. "I had finally gotten to sleep right when all this went off. Fat chance I'll be getting back to sleep tonight."

"There are pills for that, as well. Besides which, a little insomnia is nothing compared to my aches."

Gram set the book on the table and sighed. "Enough bickering. You both did a good job. Thank you. What about you, Roni? Are you okay?"

Roni stared at Gram, then Elliot, then Sully. Everything that had transpired bubbled up her throat and in a booming voice, she said, "What the fuck just happened?"

CHAPTER 3

Sully and Elliot's open-faced shock did nothing to ease Roni's swelling panic. Gram, however, snagged Roni by the ear and pulled her down into one of the chairs.

"Sit and calm down."

"How can I —"

"And watch your language, young lady. You're in enough trouble as it is."

That quieted Roni. With all that she had witnessed, she forgot that she wasn't supposed to be down there in the first place. However, being quiet and being calm were two supremely different states at the moment. Especially when Roni could see the book bumping on the table of its own accord.

Gram placed a firm hand on the cover. "Roni, look at me."

Roni lifted her eyes.

"Are you injured?"

Both men watched her carefully, and she thought all three of them held their breath waiting for an answer. She couldn't trust herself to speak. If she opened her mouth, she thought she might start babbling or screaming or something. But she managed to shake her head.

"Good," Gram said. The book bounced under her hand once more. "Sully, lock this thing down and then fix my padlock alarm on the door. Elliot, when he's done, please refile this book where it belongs."

The two old men gave quick nods and got to work. Gram put her hands on her hips and looked at the mess in the room. Shaking her head, she started pushing the chairs back where they belonged.

Sully hunched over the book. Roni watched him closely but couldn't see what he was doing. When he backed away, the book no longer moved and he had unraveled the chain around it.

Clearing his throat, he said, "All done here. Do you want to chain the spine?"

Gram gave it a moment of thought before snatching up the book. She took the chain from Sully and made a fast motion along the book's spine. As she returned to tidying up the room, Roni saw that the chain was now embedded into the middle of the spine. She leaned forward to get a better look, but Elliot swiped the book away.

As both men left the room, Gram picked up one of the tall reading lamps and reset its shade. "I'm surprised this thing survived," she said. "Never underestimate the power of dumb luck. Although, in my experience, that kind of luck usually doesn't work in your favor. This time, though, I'm glad it did — I like this lamp." She faced Roni, and her mouth tightened into a thin line. "Now, we have to deal with you."

Shrinking under her grandmother's glower, Roni glanced away. Her mind swirled in a clutter of images as fast moving as the hurricane winds from that book. Bad enough to try understanding that Darin had been sucked into a book, but trying to rectify Gram and the Old Gang with these new persona gave Roni a headache.

Gram stepped closer, looming over, and said, "This was your first date with Darin, yes?"

"What?"

With a sharp bite to her voice, Gram said, "Pay attention. You can be worried or confused or upset later. I need to know how many times you've dated Darin."

"J-Just tonight. This was our first — though, he called it our second."

"Did he threaten you? Did he threaten me?"

"No. He was fine. A little pushy. A little strange. I was uncomfortable and wanted him to leave, but he never threatened anybody."

"Then how did he get you to open the door?"

Roni looked up. "I'm fine, by the way. I wasn't hurt."

"Don't get sassy with me. I know you're fine. We already asked you that. Are you suffering memory loss?"

"No. I don't think so."

"You remember we asked if you were injured?"

With an impatient sigh that made her feel ten years old, she said, "Yes, I remember. I'm a little shaken up, that's all."

"We may not have time for you to get feeling all perfect. So, pull yourself together and answer the damn question. How did Darin get you to open the door?"

Roni flinched at Gram swearing. "I didn't open the door. He had me go for some water and when I got back, he had gone down here and smashed it open."

"I see. That's why my alarm went off. One more question — before he distracted you with the water, at any time before that, did he make a call, try to contact somebody, anything like that?"

"I don't think so."

"I need you to be sure. Did he contact anybody?"

The insanity of the evening finally flooded Roni. "I don't know! I don't know! What the hell is going on around here? How come there are caverns under our bookstore? Why is there a book that swallowed my date? And who the hell are you people?"

Breathing heavy and dabbing at her tears, Roni barely noticed Gram's hand on her shoulder. "It's going to be okay," Gram said. "Come with me."

The old woman led Roni back up into the basement and then further up to the main floor of the bookstore. She gestured to the big table and Roni sat. Gram then headed to the front counter, reached under, and produced a bottle of vodka and two shot glasses.

Despite Roni's trembling fingers, she managed to cover her mouth in surprise. "How long has that been under there?"

Gram grinned as she shuffled over to the table. "I've always kept it there — behind a sliding panel. As you're discovering tonight, this place is full of secrets." She settled in a chair next to Roni and poured two shots. "I'm sorry this happened tonight. I truly wish this all could have waited a few more years but it is what it is. I'm afraid the shocks aren't over. You need to know some more of the truth."

Roni knocked back the vodka. "I'll settle for any of the truth. None of this makes sense to me."

"I know." Gram eyed her shot glass but left it untouched. "Now, where to begin?"

"How about at the beginning?"

"That's too far back. Long before my life. Perhaps before any life began."

"Well tell me something because if you keep talking cryptically, I'm going to start screaming again."

Lacing her fingers together, Gram bumped her hands

against her chin. "The world, the universe, is more complex than most people know. It is made up of many worlds, many universes, and they are meant to be kept separate from each other. Sometimes mistakes happen. Sometimes the thin veil between worlds tears open. Elliot, Sully, and I are the repairmen."

Roni poured another shot and downed it fast. "What does any of that mean?"

"You're not listening. You're trying to find some simple explanation that will dismiss what you experienced. But that's not reality. Pay attention and understand. These rips between worlds are dangerous, and as long as humans have existed, we've had individuals who could fight back, repair the damage, and protect us all."

"And that's you and Elliot and Sully?"

"Exactly."

"Just you, or are their elderly mystic superheroes all over the world?"

"Thankfully, the world only needs the three of us. These problems don't arise too often. But when they do, we're ready. But of course, as you've pointed out, we're getting old. It's time for some new blood to learn the ropes and be ready to take over."

Roni rubbed her temples. "How is any of this possible? How could you be this person and I never knew it? And what about Darin? Is he ... is he dead?"

"I don't know yet. If he's dead, he's dead and there's nothing to do. If he's alive, he should be okay for now. Us old folks aren't mystic superheroes. At least, we don't bounce like superheroes. I'm sure those boys are every bit as exhausted as I am from this evening, and you look like you could use some sleep, too."

"Sleep? But if Darin is alive, don't we have to do something?"

"We will. But we'll be no good to him if we're too tired and weak to perform our duties."

"But —"

Gram put her palm up. "You've only learned a smidge of the real world. Don't start thinking you understand what needs to be done. Now, I've explained enough for tonight. You go home and get some sleep. I promise that if Darin is alive, we'll do everything possible to get him back. In the meantime, you have big decisions to make."

"About what?"

"For starters, whether you want to know anything more. There's a lot I can share with you, but only if you're willing to take that path where it will lead. Otherwise, I'm afraid I can't tell you anything more. You'll have to stop visiting here. I can't have you tempted to go into that room again. And, of course, you absolutely cannot tell anybody what you've learned."

"Are you going to magically wipe my brain?"

Gram chuckled. "I wish such a thing existed. That would have made my life a lot easier over the years. No, honey, nothing will stop you from telling the world except that you know the world won't believe you. In fact, they'll end up locking you away, studying you, writing papers about your mental aberrations, and in the end, you'll die stuffed in a straitjacket with your mind clouded by drugs."

"Drugs sound pretty good right now."

Placing her hand over Roni's, Gram said, "I know this a lot to take in. That's why you need to listen to your old Gram. Go home, get some rest, and decide if you really want to know all that I know, all that the world truly is. If you do want that, then you come in here tomorrow morning, and we'll show you everything. If you don't, then don't come in." She patted Roni's hand. "Now, I'm tired."

Roni knew that when Gram patted her hand after a talk,

that was the polite way of saying to get out. Still feeling wobbly — and the vodka didn't help — she walked over to the counter to gather her things together. She glanced back at the table. Gram stared at the full shot glass and did not move.

"Good night," Roni said out of habit. She left the bookstore and wondered how long Gram would stay in that chair before she finally drank the vodka.

Walking to her apartment three blocks down, Roni never saw the cars, the people, or the town. Her mind juggled everything from the terror on Darin's face to the powerful strength Gram displayed as she pulled on that chain to the way Sully protected her and never budged to Elliot's brave attempt to save Darin. She thought about the idea that there were ruptures between worlds — heck, that there was more than one world, one universe. Gram promised to save Darin, but from what? Killer books? Magic chains? How could Roni be sure that any of this was true? Three old people being the protectors of the universe? That was crazier than anything she had witnessed. And now Gram wanted her to come back and hear more. Worst of all — Roni knew that no matter how late she stayed up thinking it all over, no matter how many times her brain would toss around all she had learned, no matter if she rejected it all or accepted it as gospel, she knew she would have to go back in the morning. She had to hear the rest. No matter what it meant.

Passing a narrow alley, she leaned in and threw up.

CHAPTER 4

As the morning sun warmed Roni's face, she winced and offered a slow moan that echoed in her head. Hangovers were something she thought had ended years ago in college. It took her twelve minutes to overcome the pain and get out of bed. She spent another five minutes navigating her way around the plates on the floor she had meant to get into the overflowing sink, discarding last night's clothes onto the floor, and stumbling into the shower. After washing up, fifteen minutes passed as she rummaged through piles of dirty clothes searching for something semi-clean to wear.

Exhausted from the effort, she plopped down on the side of her bed and concentrated on breathing. To her right, she had a short bookcase with all her prized hardcovers neatly arranged alphabetically. No matter what chaos arose in her life, she could always look at that bookcase and it calmed her.

She lowered her head into her hands and closed her eyes. A full minute went by in which she held her mouth shut tight for fear of throwing up on the floor. When the feeling passed, she took a deep breath and opened her eyes.

On the floor, under a bra, she spotted the photo album — the blue one with thin lines of gold swirls painted on the front, the only one she owned. It contained the only photographs she had of her mother and father. The only memories she had of them. Most of her memories from the time of her mother's death through her teens were a fuzzy mess, but whenever she wanted a clear image of them, she had her photo album.

Gram called it Roni's "Lost Time". Doctors had looked her over, tested her, and found nothing neurologically wrong. Psychiatrists went to work and said that the trauma of her loss had created a mental block into forming new memories as clearly. They suspected that once Roni had fully come to accept all that had happened, she would be fine and the block would lift.

That sort of happened, but not exactly. As high school came around, Roni had a short but intense phase in which she delved into the world of alien conspiracies. Though her experiences with Lost Time were drastically different than alien abductees, her sense of knowing others out there suffered similar things made her feel better. By the end of her freshman year, her new experiences locked into her memory in full color, texture, and sound. Her memory worked again.

But the period of Lost Time remained. She did not get back those memories, and the ones she clung to remained faint sketches of moments.

Back on her feet, with more pep but still a headache, she dressed, picked up the album and walked into her tiny living room. She managed to drink a glass of water. She considered ditching the day and wallowing in the few memories she had of her mother. No. She had to report to the bookstore.

By the time she wrestled her hair into an acceptable

appearance and locked up the apartment, she had begun to feel close to human. Walking up toward *In The Bind*, she checked her phone for the time — another hour had gone by.

Why had Gram given her that vodka? Why had she accepted it?

Images of the cavern of weird beneath the bookstore rumbled around her head. Oh, yeah. There was that.

She inhaled the fresh morning air. If nothing else, Pennsylvania had some good, fresh air. Even living in Olburg, a small town of little note other than being within thirty minutes of Philadelphia — except now Roni would have to revise that statement. There was something of note about Olburg. Something big.

Walking along the brick sidewalk, a minefield with missing bricks and tree roots creating sudden swells in the path, Roni looked at the town as if she had never seen it before. She trudged uphill and while the neighborhood appeared pleasant enough — narrow homes lined with trees, a decent downtown within walking distance, a thriving community of artists, musicians, bankers, doctors, everything a town needed to function — yet it all seemed off.

How could all of what she had seen exist right underneath everyone's feet?

She pressed the heel of her hand against the side of her head. She could barely describe what she had seen let alone comprehend how it mixed with a town like Olburg. Gram had promised answers but as Roni walked closer to the bookstore, she wondered if she really wanted to know.

When she reached *In The Bind,* Elliot waited on the sidewalk. He leaned on his cane and offered a light wave as she approached.

"Good morning," he said. "Are you feeling okay?"

Roni smirked. "I'm a bit hungover. Gram's vodka packed a helluva punch."

He laughed. "That it does. Come walk with me. I'm going to fill you in on things."

Gesturing to the front door, she said, "Did Gram ask you to do this?"

"Your grandmother rarely asks; she orders. And yes, this is the way she wants it to be."

"She won't see me? I thought she wasn't still mad at me."

"Do not worry about that right now. You've got a big day ahead of you. Trust me on this. You need to walk with me."

Roni followed Elliot as he shambled his way further downtown. "Where are we going?"

"A quiet place that I really like."

He led her toward First Street, turned right, and kept going. Most of the shops had yet to open for the day. Roni thought that was odd considering nine o'clock had come and gone, but then she remembered her date with Darin was on Saturday night. For a Sunday morning, she was surprised to see anybody awake yet.

After two blocks, Elliot stopped at the locked door of the Ol' Olburg Gallery — a local art gallery that never opened on a Sunday. Mrs. Esther Simon owned the three-story building, renting the top two floors as apartments and running the gallery from the bottom, and she believed that Sunday was meant for prayer and nothing more.

Elliot glanced up and down the street before he leaned over the lock. He brought his hands up, closed his eyes, and murmured to himself. If he knelt on a prayer rug, Roni would have assumed he had taken up with his Muslim roots.

A soft click, and Elliot smiled. He turned the knob. The

door opened, a bell jingled from above, and he walked in.

"How did you do that?" Roni asked.

"One of my specialties. Where Sully is good at locking things, I am good at unlocking them."

"But how? You didn't use lockpicks or a credit card or anything. All I could see was you whispering to it."

"Patience. I will explain as much as I can. I promise."

He waited for Roni to enter the gallery, then he closed the door, making sure to mute the bell. A desk had been situated off to the side of the entrance. Elliot slid open one of the drawers and pulled out a key. He used this to unlock another door which led to the main hall of the gallery.

This open area had several walls of paintings and four sculptures placed at different sections of the floor. Most of the work came from local artists of varying skill levels — paintings of farmland, family pets, and even an old galleon at sea. All of it had heart. Even the least among them showed a passion to create and express through paint or sculpture.

Elliot escorted Roni to a wall filled with color swirls in a series of abstracts. "Did you understand what your grandmother told you last night? Or were you too much in shock to take any of it in?"

"A little of both. I barely slept because I couldn't stop thinking about it all."

"Perhaps this will help. Take a look at these paintings. Imagine each one as an entire universe upon itself filled with stars and planets and life. The edge of the painting is the limit of the universe. To those inside, it may seem infinite but the truth is that it does have boundaries."

"I'm not up-to-date on my physics but I'm pretty sure Einstein or Hawking or one of those guys showed that the universe curved around like a ball. You'd never reach an edge."

"I asked for you to imagine. This is not an exact replication of reality. Besides, after everything you saw last night, are you really going to fall back on Einstein?"

"You've got a point there."

Using his cane to underscore his words, Elliot continued. "Now, each one of these paintings is a universe — a place with its own physical laws, its own chemical makeup, its own everything. Sully, Lillian, and I each have been given a special gift to aid in keeping order within our universe. We are the frame around the painting. Our job is to keep our painting within its frame and make sure the others don't come into ours. Usually that is not difficult, but on occasion it happens — sometimes by accident, sometimes by a person like your Darin."

"*Special gifts?*"

"Oh, yes. You have already seen how your grandmother controls the books and the chains that bind them."

Roni nodded. "And Sully stood like a boulder."

"That is but an offshoot of his true power. You will see what he can do later today."

"And you?"

"I can touch the life essence of a soul. I can locate and heal all sorts of things. I'm also the fittest of us three, so I am often called upon to be our muscle. The older we get, the tougher our job becomes."

"You are getting older, though, right? You're not immortal or something?"

Elliot chuckled. "No. And I wouldn't want to be. When we die, there will be others to take our place. That is the way it has always been. It is not always instantaneous, but eventually a full complement will reform. I imagine there must be similar groups in the other universes as well."

"It's just you three here?"

"That is right."

Roni covered her mouth and laughed. "I always wondered how the three of you ended up together. You always seemed like the start of a bad joke — a Christian, a Muslim, and a Jew walk into a bookstore."

"You should not assume anything about us simply by those titles."

"But the Priests and the Rabbis and the Imams, they are the ones who call on you from all over the world, right? I'm thinking about all those trips you three would take. You told me that you had religious scholars and other friends around the world who would tell you about rare books they found, but that wasn't true, was it? You were going off to fight whatever had slipped through from another universe. Right?"

"The fact that you see it that way tells me you are starting to accept the truth. To answer your question — yes and no. Most of the time, yes, we were doing our jobs to protect our world. But sometimes we actually did find rare books. Sometimes both things happened. And it is not always religious leaders who contact us. It is anybody in a unique position to know the truth and be able to respond."

A moment of silence descended upon them as they observed the paintings. Roni wanted to speak or make a noise but something told her to stay quiet. From the corner of her eye, she watched Elliot. He seemed at complete peace, content to look upon the paintings and be still.

"I'm sorry," she said. "I can't act like this is all normal."

"But it is normal. What you believed to be normal before was the crazy part."

Her head throbbed waves of pain from the bottom of her skull up into the backs of her eyes. "I really shouldn't have drunk so much. I don't usually get such a bad hangover, though."

Elliot frowned. "Did your grandmother use the bottle

under the register?"

"Yeah. Why?"

"I think she was trying to help you acclimate. That bottle is a Relic with a capital R. Sometimes when we close off a tear from another universe, items fall into ours."

"Wait. Are you saying she gave me vodka from another universe?"

"I suspect so."

Roni didn't know whether to be amazed or pissed off. The latter won out. "Are we going to stand here all day or can I go back to the bookstore?"

"Not yet. You have to understand. You have to make a choice."

"I understand fine. There are countless universes out there and like these paintings, they are meant to stay separate. But that doesn't always happen. So, you three are the stopgap. You go out there, catch whatever came through and send it all back, then you plug up the hole. Right? Now, what's this about a choice?"

Elliot wagged his finger. "Not exactly right. You see, we cannot close the holes. We don't know how. That is why we have your grandmother. She creates the books. We stop the gaps by containing them into the books."

"What?" Roni had lost count of how many times her heart had skipped a beat. "Are you saying that all those breaches into our world still exist? That they're all sitting underneath the bookstore, locked away in some kind of magic books?"

"Good," he said with a broad smile. "That is correct. The cavern, the books, the chains — all of it is designed to house the tears between universes."

She tried to digest this, but then recalled the question he had yet to answer. "What about this choice? What is it you want me to do?"

All the brightness on his face faded. "This group of ours — well, we are old. When Darin broke in, it set off an alarm that Sully had placed on the padlock. We knew at that moment that somebody had gone into the caverns. Yet ..."

"It took you guys a long time to get down there."

"Yes. We were slow to hear the alarm, slow to get out of bed, slow to dress for a fight, and slow to actually reach the caverns. That is not to say that we do not have some good years still in us, but simply that we are not young people anymore. Protecting the universe tends more to the youthful side."

Roni put her arm around Elliot's waist and gave him a loving shake. "I'm sure the three of you have plenty of strength to spare."

"You know, we originally were four. My wife, Janwan, passed away."

"Because of all this?"

"No. Pancreatic cancer. Excuse my language, but fuck cancer." He leaned on his cane so that his face came in close to her. "When Janwan died, your grandmother wanted your mother, Maria, to take over. But then, unfortunately, your mother had her accident. So, we decided to keep it just us three until the time would come that we found a good match for a fourth. That time is now."

Elliot said nothing more. He stood there, staring at her. Addled by the overwhelming volume of shocks coming her way, Roni stood there staring back for a while before her eyes finally widened. "Oh. You want me?" She backed away. "No, no, no. That's not ... that doesn't make sense. Why would you want me? I don't have magic powers. I'm not ready for this kind of thing. Besides, I'm an atheist."

"Perfect! It is our respect for each other's differing opinions that we hold as one of our greatest strengths."

"I mean, everything you've said is amazing, and if I hadn't been down there and seen it all, I would have thought you were nuts, but I did see it, I did experience it all, and it is amazing. How could I turn down a chance to be part of that?"

"Exactly."

"But my life is in turmoil enough. I don't even have a job."

"The Society provides a healthy income, so you won't have to worry about that. And, best of all, you can't be fired. This is an appointment for life. Like the US Supreme Court."

"What's the Society?"

Rolling his eyes, Elliot said, "Unfortunately, this sort of universes ripping apart in each other doesn't stay hidden and secret forever. A few centuries back, the Society was formed as an oversight committee to make sure we are accountable for what we do. Mostly, it exists as a method for those in power to feel like they have some control over us. They do not. You will learn all about it when you join us."

"Hold on there." Roni glanced down the hall, part of her thinking that a good sprint away from all of this would be a smart start. "I haven't agreed to anything. This is a lot to accept."

"I do apologize for throwing it onto you this way, but Lillian insisted. After all, we do have some urgent business to get working on, and your grandmother leads our trio."

"Business? You mean saving Darin?"

"Exactly."

Roni headed toward the door. "Great. Let's put this decision of mine on the back burner and we'll go help Darin. I'm sure by the time we're done with that, I'll be able to make a choice."

Elliot did not move.

She looked back at him and crossed her arms. "Really? After everything I've seen and all that you've told me, you're going to make me choose now?"

"You should never have seen the things you did, and the only reason we decided to tell you what we have is because we feel strongly that you will join us. But the rest of the secrets we still hold will remain secrets unless you do." She started to answer but he raised a hand to shush her — too much like Gram. "I will go wait outside. Stay here a moment. Look at the paintings. Let your mind relax and open your heart to your thoughts. Only then will you know the true answer of what you want."

He walked out and Roni resisted the urge to follow. Instead, she did as he had asked. She stood there, staring at the swirls of color on the canvases, and she tried to relax. But how could she relax when the last twelve hours had been overflowing with insanity? How could she go back to her mundane existence knowing what reality truly was?

Her pulse pounded in her chest. The decision had to be based on more than a gut feeling. After all, there was a massive chasm between dreams and reality. It could be fun to dream of living the life of an international spy like James Bond — the action, the adventure, the gadgets, and the close calls — but the reality of that life would be quite different.

She thought about the Old Gang. She had known them her whole life. They never appeared to be enjoying martinis while gambling in Morocco as an undercover agent. They were quiet people, living quiet lives. She saw now that wasn't by mistake or happenstance. They had to maintain a low profile, an unassuming life, in order to keep their job a secret.

Any dreams Roni harbored of a future would disappear.

No chance for fame or fortune or maybe even happiness. Once she accepted the job, she would be in it for life. That would be it. No change of career.

And what of love? Family? How could she build a relationship with someone when she had this enormous secret to hold?

Worst of all — while there would probably be times of great excitement, her one experience already had been more terrifying than exciting. This wouldn't be fun-filled action like a movie. This would be a case of make a mistake and die.

Elliot walked up behind her. "I'm sorry to interrupt, but you've been standing here for almost an hour. If you're going to join us, we've got to get working."

An hour? Roni glanced up at Elliot, tears wetting her cheeks.

"It's okay," he said. "This life is not for most people. No need to cry. You won't be disappointing any of us."

She shook her head. "It's not that. I think I'm mourning the life I thought I would live."

"Oh?" Elliot put out his hand. "Then you'll join us?"

She nodded and shook his hand. "Let's go save Darin."

But Elliot pulled his hand back. "No, dear. I did not offer to shake hands. I need you for a little balance. I left my cane in the hall."

"Sorry," she said and set his hand on her shoulder.

Together they ambled back, picked up his cane, and left the gallery. A few people meandered outside, but nobody bothered them. Walking side by side, heading toward the bookstore, Roni's chest swelled. She couldn't help it. As much as she looked forward to helping others and protecting the universe, she kept wondering what special power they would gift to her. She kept thinking — *I'm going to have magic.*

CHAPTER 5

"You don't get a power." Gram never even glanced up from the books spread out on the main table at the bookstore.

"But all of you have powers."

Gram glared at Elliot. "How much did you tell her?"

Elliot offered a sheepish smile. "She is your family. I figured she could be trusted to know a little more than most."

"Then why does she think she gets a power?"

"I may not have mentioned all the finer details of that point."

That got Gram's attention. "Then she's here under a false assumption. Her decision to join us must be pure."

"Hey!" Roni said. "I'm standing right here."

Gram slammed her book closed and shifted in her chair to face Roni and Elliot. She rested her hands on her belly, absentmindedly fiddling with the long, beaded necklace she wore. Moving her index finger only, she pointed at Elliot. "Will you kindly go downstairs and get an update on Darin, please? We need to keep an eye on how that man is faring."

Bowing slightly, Elliot made his way toward the

basement. Gram then cocked her head towards Roni. Her eyes roved up and down as if appraising a meager painting from an unknown artist.

This was hardly the first time Roni had endured that disapproving appraisal look. Most every important milestone of her life had been met with those harsh eyes — straight As, making a new friend, first period, first love, first college acceptance, and on and on. Gram meant well — Roni told herself that many times — yet she lacked the ability to show it. Roni had always assumed it had something to do with herself, but now she wondered if the difficulties of leading a double-life or the great strains of meeting her job requirements had contributed to her hard parenting style.

At length, Gram said, "Powers are not handed out like invitations to the school dance. Everybody doesn't get one. In fact, nobody gets one handed to them. You have to earn the right to see if you are capable of gaining a power. If you pass that point, we'll discuss it further."

"How do I earn that right?"

"You spend the next several years, perhaps even decades, working with us. You do a good job, show yourself to be responsible with our secrets, and never talk back to me."

Roni squinted. "You made that last part up."

"Maybe. Are you going to risk losing a chance at a power to find out?"

Roni closed her mouth and said nothing. Then Gram laughed.

"Okay, okay," she said. "I made up that last part. But you'd be smart to listen to what I have to say. I've been doing this a long time. And before you speak up, you still have to make your choice. Now that you know you won't be given a power, at least not yet, do you wish to remain here and learn all we have to share?"

"I do. I can do this. Even without a magic power."

"We'll see."

With that Gram rocked forward and onto her feet. Brushing her backside, she headed for the elevators. "My legs are a bit achy today. You can take the elevator with me or meet me on the third floor."

Roni hustled to Gram's side and helped her into the elevator. They rode up in silence. When they reached the third floor, Gram led the way through the old room.

The cool air — always maintained at a low 64 degrees Fahrenheit — prickled Roni's arms. Four light tables dominated the center of the room for working on restoration and preservation while metal shelves held brittle, decomposing books waiting their turn. Gram ignored all of this and walked straight to the back.

Roni's skin prickled again — this time from the fear that she would see another hole in the wall leading to another hidden cavern. The fact that they were on the third floor did nothing to alter her unease. At the back wall lined with full bookshelves, Gram paused to face Roni.

"This is your last chance. I'm sure you feel like your whole world has flipped, but you know nothing compared to what I'll show in the years to come if you join us."

"I'm not turning back on this. How could I?"

Gram's head wobbled as she seemed to weigh possible answers. Finally, she pushed the spines of three books on two different shelves. An entire section of the wall slid open.

Roni grinned as she shook her head. "How many secret rooms are in this building?"

"Maybe more than I know about. Come on. Time to see Sully's workshop."

They entered a room easily as big as the one they had

left. Roni marveled that she had never noticed the third floor wasn't big enough to cover the entire size of the building, that there had to be more space beyond what she thought of as the back wall. To be fair, she rarely went to the third floor. In fact, as she thought about it, there were numerous times that one of the Old Gang went out of their way to prevent her from going to that floor — usually with the excuse of a new book in such bad condition they had to limit the number of people on the floor at any one time. Body heat, body oils, even the human breath could all be damaging to something so fragile.

Sully's workshop proved to be a marvel of its own. One giant room, ten-foot ceiling, filled with lights and all manner of equipment lining the walls. The center of the room had a grid painted on the floor and remained mostly clear except for whatever project Sully worked upon.

At the moment, this consisted of a seven-foot tall block of clay. Sully stood on an A-frame ladder as he carved away large, reddish chunks. It looked like a block head sitting atop a block body.

"What's he doing?" Roni asked.

"Didn't you pay attention to Elliot? He explained all this already."

"He didn't say anything about this."

"Sully makes Golems."

"Is that what this is?"

"It will be when he's done. Most of last night was spent getting all this clay up here. Not so easy anymore. In a few hours, he'll have enough shape carved out that we can proceed."

Sully pushed his glasses with the back of his clay-stained hands. "It won't be pretty, and it'll probably move a bit stiff, too, but it'll do the job."

Roni waved. "Do you need any help up there?"

"Not today. Thanks. Besides, we all have our assignments. This thing only works when we do our part. Now, let me get back to work or we won't be saving anybody at all."

Gram ushered Roni further across the floor until they reached the far windows. She sat on the deep ledge and scooted over to make room for Roni. "Something about these windows makes me want to smoke a cigarette."

"You smoke?"

"Not for years. But a spot like this one that's almost like a window bench, well, that gets the craving going for a bit."

Roni chuckled. "I have to say it again. This is all amazing. I still can't believe you were able to hide this from me all these years."

With a dismissive wave, Gram said, "You were more interested in your own life than mine. That's normal. You'll see it for yourself once you start having to hide this from others you know or care about. It's not too hard. Usually."

"I guess I've got a lot to learn."

The edge of Gram's lip curled upward. "That's one of the first sensible things you've said since last night. But don't worry. Elliot, in particular, is a good teacher. Sully and I will do our best, too. For now, though, you're going to have to accept a lot without question or else we'll run out of time for Darin."

Roni wanted to ask why? Did books have a time limit on them? What would happen to Darin if they passed the limit? What would happen to the book?

She opened her mouth but snapped it shut. Then, after a short breath, she said, "Tell me what I have to do."

"Your main job will be information retrieval."

"You want me to be your librarian?"

"Librarian and researcher, yes. This building houses numerous important volumes filled with lore and history

THE INFINITY CAVERNS   49

and wisdom from ages upon ages. We even have some very unique works, ones that you will never find anywhere else. On the occasions that our little group comes across something we've not encountered before — and considering what it is we do, that happens quite often — you will be required to find out whatever we need to know. Then you report it to us so that we can handle the situation properly."

Roni let it all sink in. "Oh Lord. I'm Giles."

"Who's Giles?"

"Television reference. Forget it."

"See, that is one of the reasons we need you. The world has changed around us so fast, but you are of a younger generation. You understand it better than we do. We're not idiots, mind you. I know how to use my phone for a lot more than calls, but there are plenty of ins and outs to the digital world that we've never learned. You'll be a great asset with your knowledge. Plus, you've worked around this bookstore for long enough. You know it better than you realize."

"Just to be clear — when trouble comes, you three will have me do all the legwork and then I'm supposed to sit back and let you get in on all the action."

"Nobody said saving the universe would be glamorous." Gram squeezed Roni's knee. "Baby steps, dear. Someday I'll pass on, as will Elliot and Sully. You need to learn the ropes so that you can take over and train others."

"I understand. I do. I guess after last night, I was thinking things would be more eventful right away."

"Trust me on this — you'll find plenty of excitement."

"I only meant —"

"I know what you meant," she said, her familiar bite returning. "But as usual, you never listen to everything that's told to you. I said your job was information retrieval.

Yes, librarian and researcher are two aspects of that, but they are hardly the entire job. You have to get us the information we require, even when that information is not available in this building."

Roni perked up. "Oh?"

"Those books I was reading when you came in detail the precise things we need to attempt a rescue of your boyfriend."

"He's not my boyfriend."

"Good. I don't care for him. Though we should talk a little about men and how you'll have to deal with such things in the future."

Before they could sidetrack into a conversation Roni knew she never wanted to have, she said, "The books downstairs — what am I supposed to do with them?"

"Nothing. I've already done that part of the research — in case you failed to join us. What I need you to do is acquire something of great personal value to Darin."

"Like what?"

"I don't know the boy, so I don't know what he values. That's some of the research you'll have to do."

"Okay." She grinned. "This is like voodoo or witchcraft or something."

Gram's face paled. "Don't ever say such a thing again."

"I didn't mean you were a witch or that, well, I just, I didn't mean —"

"Be quiet, dear."

"Yes, ma'am."

"Find something meaningful to Darin. Something that will touch him deeply no matter what state his mind is in when we locate him. Something that will lure him away."

"Away? From what?"

Gram huffed as she stood. With her mouth tight and thoughtful, she looked at the giant clay statue Sully worked

on. She took four small steps before glancing back at Roni.
"Pray we never find out."

CHAPTER 6

Roni left the bookstore. She walked downhill toward her apartment building where her car was parked. Part of her watched her feet moving, shocked that she could even stand after all that she had learned. Her head felt as numb and confused as if she had gone three rounds with a champion boxer. Though she knew she would do as asked, her mind still debated her new reality.

On the one hand, she had all that the Old Gang had told and shown her, plus she had her direct experience from the previous night. On the other hand, maybe she had gone batty and needed to commit herself. Maybe she was still in her apartment, passed out, dreaming all of this.

No. She could feel the sun on her face and hear her steps on the sidewalk. She smelled the air and saw the world around her as it always appeared. Not a dream.

"That's it," she scolded herself. "No more doubting. This is the way things are now."

She got into her car — a black Ford Focus that looked reasonable on the exterior and like the city dump on the interior. Old fast food wrappers, torn seats, and clumps of mud were only the start. It had once been her prize possession when she bought it used as a high school graduation gift. Almost fifteen years and two hundred twenty thousand miles later, it was little more than her mode of transportation — one she crossed her fingers would start each morning.

When the engine kicked in, a short whining sound wound up before disappearing. "That's new," she said as she leaned over to the glove compartment. Inside, she had an old bottle of aspirin. Popping two in her mouth, she dry swallowed, coughed, and buckled her seatbelt. "Okay, let's go information retrieving." She pulled onto the road.

On their date, Darin had taken her to an Italian restaurant near Philly called Mariano's Grove. He had implied it was his favorite place to eat, and without any other hint of where to start, she figured that would be her best chance to find out anything.

As she drove, her brain threatened to argue more on what reality had thrown her in the last twenty-four hours. But she pushed it away. Denying the strangeness would do nothing to change it. She had to keep moving forward. Dwelling on this would only drive her crazy whereas simply living her life would settle the bizarre world around her into a new state of normal.

At least, she hoped that was what would happen.

Besides, doing things the way Gram suggested meant that Roni would have a job, an income, a chance at a life. And maybe it would be fun. She never thought she would get to be a detective, yet that was exactly her duty this morning. Retracing the steps of a victim in order to help save him.

That sounded good to her ears. She could work with that.

Mariano's Grove was in the town of Exton just off of Route 30. The building had once been a chain restaurant that went out of business. Mariano bought it, refurbished it to give the place a warmer feel, and starting plating recipes from his family that reached all the way back to a little town in Italy. All of which created a fantastic atmosphere for that first date.

But under the Sunday afternoon sun, without the candlelight or wine, Roni saw the flaws more than anything — the threadbare carpet, the constant clatter in the kitchen, the bored waiters, and the inattentive hostess. In fact, Roni waited at the front counter for ten minutes before being helped. When the hostess realized Roni wasn't a customer, she plastered on a fake smile and said she had to go on break.

"Don't mind her," one of the waiters said. "It's not personal. She's always bitchy."

Roni winked. "I thought maybe I smelled bad or something."

The waiter, a tall black man with a dazzling smile, said, "You seem fine to me."

"Maybe you can help me out. I was here last night on a date, and I want to do something nice for the guy. He told me this was his favorite restaurant, that he came here a lot, so I thought maybe you guys might know a little something about him. What he likes. That kind of thing."

"I wasn't here last night. Didn't see you."

"His name's Darin Lander."

"Oh, sure. Everybody knows Darin. Comes in here every week, sometimes twice. Good tipper, too."

She faked a bit of embarrassment. "It was just our first date, and we didn't talk a lot about him. I tried, but he was very tight-lipped." As she realized her "lie" actually was true, her face reddened for real. How had she managed to go through an entire date and only talk about herself?

"What is it you want to know? I won't give you his

address or credit card info or anything like that."

"No, no. I'm going to see him tomorrow night for our second date. This time it's my turn to plan the thing, but I don't even know what he does for a living. If he's a pastry chef, I don't want to take him to a bakery."

"He's a lawyer."

"Really?"

"Oh, yeah. Works with Page Brothers. You know them, right? They've always got those commercials on TV with the guy in a full-body cast."

"Yeah, I know the one." So, Darin was a low-level ambulance chaser. "Thanks. You've helped me out so much."

"No problem." He paused, then rested his arm on the wall to show off his muscular frame. "You know, if it doesn't work out, I'd be happy to give you my number."

Roni smiled. "I'll keep that in mind." As she left, the smile drifted away. She had no interest in a man who asked her out knowing that she was dating another man. But she had to admit that her chest filled with flattered pride. Getting asked out like that never happened to her. She didn't have the classic beauty features that drove men to do crazy things. Perhaps, in part, she exuded more confidence because she now had a job, had a purpose. *Or perhaps he was hard up and thought I'd be easy.*

She got back in her car and pulled out her phone. Page Brothers' offices were in Paoli, only a few minutes from Exton and quite close to Olburg.

When she arrived at the law offices, two men in business suits hustled from office to office. They fluttered papers at each other, made phone calls, and grumbled. The receptionist gazed up from her bulky computer — a leftover from seven years ago — and asked, "What do you need, honey?"

"I'm here about Darin Lander."

The two men in the back froze. One, a pudgy fellow with a waxy mustache, rushed over. "You've seen Darin? Where is he? He never showed up. What do you know about it? Is he hurt? He better be hurt or we'll kill him."

The other man, slightly older with deep wrinkles around his eyes, approached. "Forgive my brother. We're floundering a bit by Darin's unexpected absence. It all just happened a few hours ago and we've had to reschedule a lot. You can imagine the courts will not be too cooperative with us tomorrow if we are unprepared."

"So," the first brother said, "do you know where he is or don't you?"

"That's a bit complicated," Roni said. As the words left her mouth, she wondered why she hadn't simply answered *No.*

"Complicated? What's complicated about it? Is he in some trouble? I knew he had been chatting it up with some odd people lately, but I didn't get the sense that they were trouble. I mean, he's not dealing drugs or doing anything stupid like that. Is he?"

"No, no. Nothing like that. He's, um," she said, and decided she might as well go all-in, "he's working a side project. One that might bring you all quite a bit of money."

That got the older brother's full attention. "Are you the client?"

"I'm only the messenger. A private firm needed somebody with his skills to handle a sensitive matter. The people I work for are quite secretive and they didn't give Mr. Lander a chance to contact you. I apologize I wasn't here sooner this day, but it took me a while to find you."

"Why didn't Darin tell you where we are?"

"Like I said, I'm only the messenger. I've never even seen Mr. Lander, and I was given nothing more than a name."

The first brother huffed. "You couldn't find our address online with his name?"

Roni wanted to smack herself. She was so spun around by recent events, she forgot to do the most basic thing possible. She didn't even google the guy. "The people I work for are finicky about their privacy. They shun employee internet usage."

"Doesn't seem a sensible way to run a business. What business are your bosses in, anyway?"

She raised her palms out. "I'm not at liberty to say anything more."

"I'd say you're done there then. You've delivered the message. At least, we don't have to worry about Darin's well-being now. But that doesn't make the day any easier. Excuse us. We have a lot of cleaning up to do because of this mess."

"Of course." Roni snapped her fingers. "One more thing, though. If you don't mind, I was told to fetch a few items from his office."

The older brother said, "Fine, fine. Don't take any case files out of here, though. We need those."

With nothing more, the Page Brothers returned to their bustling. Roni quietly entered Darin's office — wood panel walls, a beaten couch, and a fake fern. She couldn't believe it had been so easy to get in there. Of course, the brothers were in a state because of Darin's unplanned absence, but the way they accepted her story flummoxed her. Then again, greed could motivate a lot of poor choices, and she had seen it on both men's faces — they hoped that Darin's side project would reward the firm with plenty of high paying business. After all, who else but rich people had sensitive, secret jobs for lawyers?

Despite the gullibility of the Page brothers, Roni did not

want to push her luck. She needed to be quick. Eventually, one of the lawyers would get an idea in his head that she might be lying.

She scanned over Darin's desk — stapler, laptop, stacks of files and papers, a fancy pen in a fancy stand, nothing that suggested an item of personal importance. She checked the drawers — nothing but files, office supplies, and a bottle of brandy. Roni's stomach churned at the thought of alcohol.

Gazing at the walls, she noted the bland paintings — the kind of thing found in hotel rooms. In fact, everything about Darin's office suggested he was a bland human being without any defining characteristics. It felt strange and invasive to be combing through his life this way — especially after having been on a date with the man — but the Old Gang needed this object. Darin needed it.

Except I've got nothing.

Great. Her first assignment would end in failure. She could already see Gram's disappointed expression.

Roni's eyes shifted downward. On the desk, she saw a large calendar planner that doubled as a large blotter. Sliding the laptop to the side, her finger traced the daily notes Darin had made. Client names, times, and phone numbers had been meticulously written into the correct boxes for the days of the month. And one week away, circled and given an exclamation point, were the words *Mom's Birthday!* Whether out of habit, a touch of OCD, or because he truly needed to be reminded, he had written the phone number next to the entry.

Roni stored the number into her phone and extricated herself from the offices as quietly as possible. The Page Brothers never bothered to acknowledge her as she walked by, and even the receptionist simply nodded without looking up from her computer.

Once she had safely returned to her car, Roni brought up the number on her phone. She thought about calling but it would be too easy for Darin's mother to get suspicious and hang up. It would be far more difficult in person. Not wanting to make the same mistake twice, Roni brought up her browser and with a few searches on some basic phone directories, aided by the benefit that Darin's mother used a landline, Roni had an address in Lancaster.

"Of course," Roni said to the phone. "You couldn't bother to live nearby."

Ninety minutes later, Roni drove into a seasoned development off of Lititz Pike. She parked in front of a gray house with brick trim, walked up to the door, and rang the bell. When an elderly woman with more wrinkles on her face than teeth in her mouth answered, Roni said the first thing that came to mind. "Hi. I'm Darin's girlfriend."

CHAPTER 7

The woman's eyes sparkled as she opened the door wider and waved Roni in. Waddling like a penguin, she rushed off down a hall and returned with teeth in her mouth. "Oh my, I'm so embarrassed. I didn't know you were coming. Darin didn't say a thing. That rascal is forever letting things surprise me."

The house was immaculate — not a speck of dust on the coffee table, not a mismatched pillow on the couch, not a single picture askew on the walls. The carpet still bore lines from recent vacuuming. Even the plants looked vibrant as if freshly watered.

"Come, come," Darin's mother said. "Have a seat."

Roni settled on the edge of a couch cushion. She feared sitting fully into the couch and messing up the perfectly smooth cushions.

"Mrs. Lander —"

"Please, call me Jane."

"It's a pleasure to meet you, Jane."

Jane eased next to Roni. She was a hefty, small woman with a confident swagger behind her words. Not at all like Darin had described her. "Are we having dinner tonight?

Darin hasn't bothered to call me in a few days. He can be so forgetful."

Roni coughed to stall an answer. She had forgotten to plan a lie again, and this time there would be no business or money distraction like with the Page Brothers law firm. "I don't think so," she said. "At least, he didn't mention it to me."

"Get comfortable with that. He's very spur of the moment."

Roni glanced around the room for something that might lead her to the item she sought, but everything she spotted belonged to an old woman, not a young man. On the fireplace mantle, she saw framed photos lined up. Most were of Jane Lander as a young woman or a middle-aged mom and most had a taller black man standing with her.

"Is that Darin's father?"

Jane smiled as she gazed at the photos. "Patrick. He was a great man. Died too young, though. Only fifty-seven. Heart attack."

"He's handsome."

"Did you lose somebody early, too?"

Roni's hand went to her chest. "My mother. How did you know that?"

"Because when I told you Patrick was dead, you didn't say you were sorry. People who have lost somebody early in life learn that there's no need to say that. It doesn't help." With a gentle tap on Roni's knee, Jane said, "How rude of me. I didn't offer you anything. Can I get you a cup of coffee? Are you hungry?"

"No, thank you. I'm fine."

"Are you sure? I don't mind. It's not often that Darin brings home a girlfriend. Where is he anyway?"

"I guess he's still at work. You know how it is with lawyers."

Jane turned her head to the side and peeked back at Roni. "I wouldn't really call him a lawyer. I mean, he's not arguing difficult cases or anything. He won't be in front of the Supreme Court."

"He's got to start somewhere." Roni didn't want to think about how she found herself in the position of defending Darin. She tried to stay focused on the goal — a deeply personal item. "Do you know where we'll be eating? It seems food is kind of important to him."

With a worn expression, Jane lowered her head. "Please, don't try to fool an old lady."

"Pardon me?"

"You know, when I was younger, I could play this game all night long. I'd lie to myself and to the girl sitting where you are, and I'd promise that he surely just got caught in traffic or perhaps an emergency happened at work. If I really liked the girl, I'd even take her out to dinner. Sometimes they were so naïve, they really thought Darin would call soon to apologize. But as you get old, you get to a point where you're done with all the nonsense of life — the so-called courtesies that really are nothing more than lies we tell to avoid being honest with each other. So, why don't you tell me why you're really here? You afraid Darin is cheating on you?"

"Um ... I ..."

"Too blunt for you?"

"No. It's actually refreshing."

"Take some advice. Go find another man. I love my son. I truly do. But there's something not right with him. He doesn't handle relationships well. I'm telling you this because you look about his age, and I know thoughts of marriage are coming up in his head more and more lately. I think he thinks I need grandkids. What do I want with a bunch of dirty little tykes messing up my house? But he thinks it, and once he gets something in his head, it's hard to get him to change course. Thing is — he's not the marrying type. He won't do well with that kind of responsibility. It breaks my heart to say all this. I want him to be happy, but I have to be honest. If you're thinking he's the one — and at your age, I understand the pressure to settle down — well, go find another. He's not the one."

As Jane went on exposing the flaws of her son, Roni could see the future painted before her. A full, normal life complete with marriage and children that, apparently with Darin, also included infidelity, heartbreak, and eventually divorce. On the previous night, while dining with Darin, she had an ideal future vision running through her head. Either one could have happened. If it hadn't happened, she figured she would have been headed to plenty of lonely nights and a lot of cats.

But then the world changed. And as Roni sat there listening to Darin's mother, she could only think about how happy she had been all afternoon. Once her hangover had cleared, she found the day exhilarating. Even if she never got a special power, even if all she ever did for the Old Gang was look up information in books and go on the occasional excursion to find an object or two, the whole experience thrilled her. The drab world she had lived in had been flipped on end, and she found herself feeling an odd sensation deep inside — gratitude.

An idea sparked, and she put out her hand to clasp Jane's. "I appreciate everything you've said. But I'm afraid I'm in love with him. I can't turn back. I think about him all the time, and well, like you suspected, I came here because I think I might be losing him." It scared Roni a little at how easily the lies came. "Please, Jane, please. I've heard what you're saying, but I also know what's in my heart. I think I need to — no, I know it — I've got to try to win him back.

If it's meant to be, then it'll happen. If I fail, I'll listen to your warning. But I've got to try."

Jane covered their entwined hands with her other hand. "Well, I must say that I like you a lot. You've got what we used to call grit. If you're determined to be miserable with my son, then at least I'll get to have you as a daughter-in-law. That much I think I'll enjoy."

"There won't be a wedding if I don't get him back on my side."

"You came here for advice on that?"

"I was thinking that I'd do something special for him. I want to take something that he cherishes, something personal to him that would fill him with feelings of love and connection, and I'll make it special, and then give it as a present. I want to show him that I really understand him."

Jane's face brightened. "I know the perfect thing." She crossed the room to a low bookshelf and lifted out a heavy photo album. Beaming as she returned to the couch, she said, "You know I think you're a bit crazy to stay with him, but the idea that I will have you in my life is wonderful. Before you say anything — I know we've only met, but I've seen enough of Darin's girlfriends. I can tell. You're something special. Your honesty alone is a significant improvement."

Roni tried to hide her discomfort. "I'm sure you'll find my flaws eventually. That's even if I can get him to stay with me."

"Oh, he will. He's an idiot but he's not that much of an idiot. Oh, you wouldn't believe how many lying little tramps I've met. And for what? They think because he's a lawyer that he's rich. But you — you don't strike me as a gold digger."

"He made it clear to me from the start that he wasn't rich."

"Did he?"

Roni cleared her throat. She tried to recall the things Darin had talked about on their only date. Maybe he hadn't said anything so bold. Well, since Jane appreciated straight talk, Roni figured that would be the best approach. "I don't remember now. I could have sworn he said something like that, but then maybe it was more of an impression."

"Probably. While I wouldn't expect him to brag about money he doesn't have, I don't think he'd go out of his way to diminish himself either."

Roni let a short silence slip between them and kept her eyes on the photo album. Jane took the hint well. She flipped through several pages until she reached one that had a photo of Darin in his twenties sitting with his father courtside at a 76ers game. Two tickets stubs were next to the photo.

"It was a gift for graduating law school," Jane said, peeling back the plastic and removing one of the ticket stubs. "Patrick and I were so proud. We wanted to do something special, but we could only afford two tickets. So, we went out to dinner as a family and then the boys went to watch basketball. The two of them talked about that game for a week after it happened. I think it was the closest they ever felt together. It was also the last big thing they ever did. Three months later, Patrick died."

When Roni took the ticket stub, she swore she could feel energy coming off it. However, she also knew that her pulse quickened under the pressure of her lies. She wanted to grab hold of Jane's shoulders, look her deep in the soul, and tell her that Darin was in trouble, that his life was threatened, but not to worry. A great team had assembled to save him.

Great team. Sure. Three geriatrics and an unemployed slacker.

"Thank you," she said. "I'll make sure to take good care of this."

"Please do. I have a strong feeling that he's going to love whatever you do."

"You've been very kind to me, Jane."

"No, no. Let's be perfectly positive about this. You call me Mom."

Roni blushed. "I'll try."

Jane laughed. "Good luck now."

After a few more pleasantries, Roni hurried back to her car and headed for Olburg. During the first half of the drive, she periodically burst into triumphant shouts followed by giddy laughter. She had succeeded. First day on the job and she had succeeded. She had started with nothing more than a name and a restaurant, and by the end, she had retrieved the ticket stub, met Darin's mother, learned a lot of possibly valuable information about Darin, and been invited to join the family.

As the sun lowered and sent annoying orange rays glaring in her rearview mirror, Roni exited the highway. A few minutes later, she parked out front of the bookshop. Eager to see Gram's face when she handed over the ticket stub, Roni almost forgot to lock her car — even a monstrous piece of junk could get stolen.

When she entered the store, her proud smile vanished. Gram slumped on the floor with her back against the endcap of a bookshelf — her eyes wide, her face pale, and her hand clutching her chest.

CHAPTER 8

Roni shot across the room and slammed onto her knees beside Gram. "Hold on. I'm here now. I'm going to call for help. Just hold on."

She fumbled out her phone. Under trembling fingers, she dialed 9-1-1. This couldn't be happening. After all she had learned in the last day, after her world had been upended, it would be the cruelest joke to rip apart her family again. Salty tears flowed into her mouth.

"Why aren't they answering?" she yelled.

She looked at the phone and saw that she had forgotten to press SEND. Before she could raise her thumb toward the green icon, Gram's hand batted at the phone.

"No," Gram said.

"You need an ambulance and the paramedics. I don't know any first aid to help you."

"They can't help me." Straining through her pain, she added, "Get ... Elliot."

"But —"

"Get Elliot!"

The urgency of Gram's voice cut straight through Roni's brain. Nodding like a bobble-head, she pressed the phone into Gram's hand and dashed to the stairwell. The elevator would be too slow.

She bolted up flight after flight until she reached the top floor. Both the stairs and the elevator opened into a tiny lobby big enough for the doors to the two apartments and two chairs to sit while waiting for the elevator. Roni went to the right — Elliot and Sully's apartment — and banged on the door.

"Elliot! Elliot!" Why wasn't he answering? He always spent the early evening in prayer and almost always in his apartment. At least, she always thought he was praying. But then, she never saw him being observant of the Muslim traditions. Still, he should have been in his apartment. Did something different happen today or was he asleep? She slammed her fist against the door over and over. "Wake up! Elliot! Gram needs you!"

She heard a muffled sound from inside followed by the locks on the doors clicking. Elliot opened the door looking confused. "What are you doing making all this fuss when I'm trying —"

"Gram's having a heart attack!"

She had never seen Elliot move so fast. He dashed back into his apartment and returned seconds later with his cane — though he never let it touch the ground. He rushed down the stairs faster than Roni could keep up, pivoting on the landings like a youthful athlete, and sometimes skipping a stair.

At the bottom, he soared to Gram's side. When Roni caught up, she saw that perspiration covered his face. He had pushed himself harder than he should have, and Roni worried he might have a heart attack as well.

He held his cane parallel over Gram's body, closed his eyes, and murmured words Roni could not identify. His free hand caressed the air between Gram and the cane.

Roni watched — unable to breathe, unable to move. Elliot continued to pass his hand back and forth at a steady pace.

A golden light appeared in the air around Elliot's moving hand. At first, it looked like sunshine cutting in on a summer day — light, breezy, and warm. But then Roni spotted pinpoints of light that moved within the general glow. Fireflies of energy that swarmed around Elliot's hand.

Elliot shifted his side-to-side motion to an up-and-down one as if fanning the air. The energy descended like glowing ash. When it touched Gram's skin, it disappeared within her, absorbed like water droplets on a dry cloth. As fast as it happened, Gram's color returned to her skin, her breathing eased, and all impressions of pain left her face.

Sitting back, Elliot sighed. "She's going to be okay."

Roni stared at these two people like they were aliens. "How?"

"I heal people. That is my main gift. I thought I told you that."

"Maybe you did. But there's a big difference between hearing something like that and seeing it actually happen."

Dabbing at his forehead with his sleeve, he said, "I'm surprised you look so astounded — after what you saw last night."

"Me, too. But I am." She crouched next to Elliot and wrapped her arms around him. "Thank you." He had a comforting, smoky aroma as if he had a wood-burning stove in his apartment. "Thank you for saving her."

Gram sat up and rolled her shoulders. "It isn't the first time."

Roni tried to ease Gram back down. "Lord woman, lay down. You've got to rest."

"I've lived more decades than you. I think I know what my body needs and doesn't need." Gram shoved Roni's arms away. "Elliot's been bringing me back from near-death more times than I care to remember. So, if you want to be a help, then quit pushing me and start helping up to my feet."

Elliot took one arm and Roni the other. Together, they lifted Gram up and placed her in a seat at the big table. "She will be fine," Elliot said.

"It goes with the territory," Gram said. "After you put in a few dozen years or so on the job, you'll have been exposed to all sorts of stuff."

"Exposed?" Roni didn't like the sound of that. "Like radiation?"

"Sure. Maybe. I don't know. Each one of those books in the cavern contains a rip into another universe. You think that's benign? Every single universe is going to have its own unique bacteria, unique air mixture, unique properties of everything. There's no way you can do this work and not inhale a bit of another universe. That has lasting consequences."

"You're saying you had a heart attack because of germs from another universe."

Gram drummed her fingers on the table. "Now you're starting to see. Except in this case, no. I had a heart attack because I'm in my seventies and I've had a bad ticker for a long time. Partly old age. Mostly bad genes. If it weren't for Elliot, I'd have died ten, maybe twenty years ago. He's also saved Sully's life a few times."

Roni kissed the side of Elliot's head. "Thank you."

He leaned on his cane, wincing but trying to hide it. "Nothing to thank me for. Keeping us healthy and running is part of my job. But there are limits to what I can do." He leveled his eyes on Gram. "And how often."

Gram waved him off. "I know, I know. He's implying that soon he won't be able to stop the natural order of things. Nobody gets to cheat Death, after all. Elliot can stop me from croaking to a heart attack, but he can't stop old age. Eventually, my body's going to have had enough."

"My body, too." He shifted on his feet, once more tightening his face with the movements. To Roni, he said, "I can summon a lot of energy from the air to give myself a boost, but as I get older, it takes more and more from me."

Roni said, "Is that how you ran down the stairs like a twenty year old?"

"That's right. But my body doesn't like it. If I die before I have a successor, this group will be in serious trouble for a while. Eventually, you'll find somebody, but that doesn't mean you won't suffer in the meantime."

"Are you suggesting that I —"

Both Elliot and Gram laughed. "Not at all," he said. "You've gotten your job. But this team of four needs more youth than just you. Eventually, that is."

"That's right." Gram used the table to prop herself up to a standing position. "Eventually means later — much later. Let's deal with right now. We've got work to do. Roni? Did you get what you were assigned to find?"

Without intending to do so, Roni stepped forward with her chest puffed up. She lifted her head like a Greek warrior returning from battle under the cheers of the people, and she pulled the ticket stub from her pocket. Adding a final flick to the stub, she presented it with a reverent nod.

Gram picked it up and checked over both sides. "It's rather small."

"You never said anything about the object having to be large."

Elliot snickered. "Come on, give the girl a break. You know very well size doesn't matter. Not for this."

"Don't get saucy," Gram said without any mirth. "Particularly in front of my granddaughter."

Roni didn't know whether to laugh or scream. She opted for a third choice. She snatched the ticket stub back and asked in a firm voice, "Will it do or won't it?"

"As long as it is a deeply personal object to Darin, it'll do fine."

"Then this will be perfect."

Gram weighed Roni's confident words. "I hope you're right."

Apparently almost dying did nothing to quell Gram's rough side. As Roni pocketed the stub, she said, "Is there anything else you need from me?"

"Oh, yes." Gram's eyes blazed and her voice uttered words with dark intent. "Endless things." Then she rubbed her back like an accountant stretching from a long day pouring over financial statements, and in a pleasant tone, she said, "But for tonight's work, this will do. Sully should be ready. Elliot and I will go downstairs to prepare. Please be a dear and help Sully. He sometimes needs a hand."

Threading her arm around Elliot's arm, Gram rested her head on his shoulder. She hoisted her big bag, and the two ambled off toward the elevator with all the warmth and closeness decades of friendship could create. For a fleeting moment, Roni's tension evaporated under that warmth.

Until Gram circled her finger in the air. "Hup, hup. I don't want to be awake all night waiting for you and Sully to get downstairs."

As Roni trudged up the stairs, she muttered, "Almost dying sure has made you cranky." Thankfully, Gram did not respond.

On the third floor, Roni walked back into Sully's workshop. The Golem stood in the center of the room. It appeared like a giant figure made of simple shapes — a square block head, a cylinder body, cylinder arms, and thick rectangular legs. The head had two divots for eyes and a carved outline for a mouth. Sully ate a turkey sandwich at one of his desks.

"Are we ready?" he asked as Roni entered.

"Gram and Elliot are preparing things downstairs. She asked that I come help you."

"Not much left to do. I have to wake him up, and then we'll all go down together."

She gazed up at the clay thing. "Are they always so plain looking? I'm sorry. I didn't mean that to sound like an insult."

Wiping his hands on his shirt, Sully said, "You're wondering why, if I've been working all day on this, doesn't it look better."

"That's horrible of me. I'm so sorry."

"It's a valid question." Sipping from a straw stuck in a soda can, he pulled over a thin strip of white paper and a pen. After stifling a soda belch, he started to write in Hebrew. "It all has to do with the purpose of the Golem. Some purposes require more time than others. This one needs to be able to withstand some powerful forces. It doesn't need to look pretty. So, I put my efforts into the things you can't really see on the outside."

He adjusted his glasses, looked over what he had written, and seemed satisfied with the result. He then rolled the paper into a tight tube about the length of his fingernail. Scooting off a metal stool, he walked toward the ladder beside the Golem.

"Can I help you?" Roni asked.

"Wait there," he said and climbed the ladder. At the top, standing next to the Golem's head, he leaned out, holding onto the ladder with one hand.

Roni rushed over and steadied the ladder with her body. She arched her head back to watch, ready to attempt to catch Sully if he fell. Of course, if he fell, she figured they would both end up in the ER getting stitches, but what else could she do?

Sully placed the rolled up paper with Hebrew writing into the Golem's mouth. Then he swung over to the side and whispered into the thing's ear — not that he had made an ear, but that was the position where an ear should have been. When he finished, he climbed down.

"Don't dawdle now," he said, taking Roni's arm and guiding her toward the entrance.

As she walked away, she chanced a glance back and froze. The Golem moved. The giant, barely-sculpted chunk of clay stepped forward and thudded toward them.

Sully gave a short wave. "Good evening, there. You should take the elevator down. Much easier than the stairs. We'll meet you in the Specials Room. Did I write that part down for you?" The Golem's head nodded in an exaggerated up-and-down motion. "Good. We'll see you there."

"That's amazing," Roni managed.

"Far from my best work," Sully whispered. "But don't let him hear that. He's going to do a great service for us."

"W-What's he going to do?"

"Help us with Darin, of course. Come on. Time to save your boyfriend."

As Roni followed Sully toward the stairs, his words sunk in. "He's not my boyfriend!"

CHAPTER 9

Roni paused at the door to the caverns. The last time — the only time — she had gone through that door, her entire world had changed. After seeing all that the Old Gang could do, after learning the truth about reality from them, and after watching a slab of clay move on its own, she could not be sure that another massive change to her life did not wait beyond that entrance.

"Come, now," Sully said, but then he met her eyes. He pulled over a chair, sat, and crossed his legs. Clutching his knee, he said, "I understand."

"You do? I don't."

"I was exactly the same when I learned the truth. I'd think I had it straight in my head, I'd think I had arrived at acceptance, and then poof! All the doubts, all the fears, all the confusion threatened to drown me. It would take all my will and some kind words from those who knew, and I'd overcome the feeling, reassured that I understood the truth, the reality around me, and that I could handle it. A few days later, sometimes only a few hours later, poof! Here comes that tidal wave of worry once again. Took me about a week to fully adjust."

"A week?"

"But after that I was perfectly fine."

Out of frustration, and with a touch of defiance, Roni threw open the door and marched into the caverns. The temperature dropped. Sully's scuffling feet echoed from behind her.

"You ought to let me lead the way," he grumbled. "Too many bad directions to go in if you don't know where you're headed."

Roni waited for Sully to catch up. She wanted to storm off and decide for herself where things should happen, but Sully was right. Besides, already nothing looked familiar. Getting lost would not be an ideal way to finish her first full day at work.

Sully led her around one rock wall, then another. Each one had books chained into their shelves. This time, however, Roni understood that each book contained a tear in reality, an opening into another universe.

"There are so many," she said.

Sully's head made a short turn as he scanned across the walls. "People have been doing this for a long time. Sometimes I think we're no better than the old Dutch boy with his finger in the dam. But I suppose we should consider ourselves lucky."

"How so?"

"The dam hasn't burst yet. Some generation down the road will have to deal with that problem. But if we can hold it off another few decades, I'll be dead. Won't be my problem anymore."

"Isn't that a bit morbid?"

"Not at my age. Nobody likes to talk about dying, but when you get into your seventies, your eighties, and Lord-willing, your nineties, well you can't really deny what's coming your way. All my friends are gone except for Elliot and Lillian. The only reason we're still here is because of Elliot. You know about what he can do, yes?"

"Yeah, I know." Had Elliot really saved Gram's life less than a half-hour ago? It felt like years.

"That's that, then. Not much else I can say. We're old people and we won't live forever." He stopped, looked back, and winked. "But we're gonna cause a helluva ruckus on our way out."

After a few more passageways, Sully brought them to a metal door. They stepped inside to an entirely empty room save for a podium near the center. Carved from a stalagmite that spread into the ground, the podium had two thick chains locked into its side. No furniture or lamps or anything loose could be seen. Two lights embedded in the walls provided illumination.

A long strip of metal ran around the room at shoulder-height. Elliot and Gram stood at one wall facing the strip. Gram hefted her big bag as she adjusted her robe — a long sleeved piece like something out of an old martial arts movie.

With a flick of her hand, a thin chain dropped from the sleeve. Elliot took hold of it and connected it to rings welded into the metal strip. Three more chains had already been attached. Gram looked up as Sully and Roni entered.

Before Gram could speak, the heavy footsteps of the Golem thumped in the air. She smiled. "Sounds like you made a good one for this job."

"Of course I did," Sully said, straightening his collar.

"Make sure everyone is set. I'll get the book."

With barely a glance at Roni, Gram left the room. The thumping grew louder, and in a few seconds, the Golem ducked its head as it entered.

"Wait there." Sully pointed toward the podium, and the Golem walked over and stood at its side.

Roni had a dozen questions in her head — a number which could easily grow into a million — but she kept silent and observed. That seemed to work better with this group. Sure enough, Sully waved her over toward the wall.

"Do like me," he said.

He picked up one of the chains. Roni did the same. He took the free end and wrapped it around his waist like a belt. She did the same. He pinched the tip of the chain and it snapped open like a snake's mouth. She did, too.

"This is called the dead end." With his free hand, he pulled on the part of the chain secured to the wall. "This is the live end. Got it?"

Roni nodded. He then clamped the dead end onto the live end. It cinched along his waist, and he let out a light huff. Roni followed suit. Her chain tightened fast but stopped short of being uncomfortable.

Sully walked over to Elliot and whispered something. Roni ignored them. She had enough to digest without worrying about things they wanted to keep secret.

She tugged on the thin chain. For such a small thing, it sure appeared to hold well. But anything built to handle weight or stress was only as strong as its weakest point. The chain might be stronger than it looked, but what about the metal strip? She searched along the strip to locate how it fastened to the wall, but before she could find an answer, Gram returned.

Sully and Elliot grew still as Gram walked with solemn steps to the podium. As she set the book on the podium and undid the chains around the book, she moved with reverential grace. Roni half-expected organ music to start playing. Gram took the open chains and attached them to those chains embedded into the stone podium. She then walked to the wall and went through the same procedure Sully had instructed Roni in. When finished, all four of them had secured themselves to chains connected with the metal strip in the wall.

With a nod from Gram, Elliot stepped in front of Roni. He adjusted the chain around his belt so that it did not get tangled with Sully's. Easing Roni with a smile, Elliot said, "The ticket stub, please."

She pulled it out, and he turned her hand over, setting the stub on her palm. He then inhaled slow and deep, exhaling with a satisfied and audible sigh. "Ready?" he asked.

"No," Roni said. "But you might as well do whatever you're going to do anyway."

He held his cane at the middle and raised it to the same height as the ticket stub. With his other hand held straight upward, he drew a circle in the air, going completely around Roni's hands. First one direction, then the other. Back and forth. Clockwise and counter-clockwise. Over and over.

She first noticed the aroma. Similar to Elliot's wood fire smell, she gave it little thought, but as he continued to encircle her hands, the smell grew stronger. A rich, musky scent like a humble cabin in the mountains. Then she felt the air warm around her fingers as if she held them over a campfire. Finally, the light surrounding her hands altered — shifted into a pleasant amber.

Elliot touched the top of his cane to the light and stopped making circles with his hand. The light held to the cane like a balloon statically stuck to a sleeve. He plucked the ticket stub from Roni's hand, and placed it in the light. Floating like a gliding butterfly, it hovered in that light with majestic grace. Roni's heart leaped. It was beautiful. Elliot made a graceful bow of his head and gently stepped toward the Golem.

But a few steps short, he stopped. With an incredulous look, he turned toward Sully. "You didn't give it any hands."

"There wasn't time, and it was more important that he have the structural build to —"

"Without hands, it cannot hold the ticket stub."

Speaking in a slow growl, Sully said, "He doesn't need hands. The ticket only has to be on his body."

Elliot glanced at the Golem. "It doesn't have anything to put the stub on."

"Oh, for crying out loud," Gram said. "Sully, fix it."

Grumbling as he crossed over, Sully gave Elliot a slight push out of the way. He snapped his chain aside and approached the Golem. "Sorry about this," he said. He jabbed his hand into the Golem's side — right where the appendix would be, if it were human — and scooped out some clay. Making a grand bow, he said, "Will that suffice, your Highness?"

Elliot did not take the bait. He simply strode forward and used the cane to set the ball of light with the ticket stub into the hole Sully had created. "How do we keep the ticket from falling out?"

As if staring at an incompetent student, Sully slapped the clay he held back over the hole. "Your ticket doesn't need to be visible." He scurried back to his spot on the wall with a smirk on his lips.

Elliot scowled but did not provoke the situation further — probably because of the sharp look Gram sent his way. Instead, he took up his position and paused to make eye contact with each person. Each time, with Gram and then Sully, they nodded back at him. When he looked to Roni, she nodded, too — a bit vigorous, but she did nod.

"Let's get on with this. Darin can't wait forever." Sully said. To Roni, he added, "This guy can be so dramatic."

"Very well." Elliot reached out toward the book with his cane and flipped the cover open.

As had happened before, the room depressurized. Air sucked into the book at typhoon speeds. If not for the chains around their waists, the whole team would have fallen in.

Gram cupped her mouth and yelled each word slowly. "We only have about ten minutes before these chains give way. Get that thing moving."

Sully gave her a thumbs-up. He then made a series of gestures at the Golem which Roni could not follow. The Golem stomped across the room. Its size and weight kept it anchored to the floor despite the winds whipping around it. When it reached the podium, the Golem raised its leg high and stepped into the book like one might step into a bathtub with a tall side.

For several seconds the gale died down as the Golem blocked much of the path for the air to enter the book. A high-pitch whined while the Golem lowered itself deeper. Roni opened her mouth to ask how long the Golem could handle such strong winds, but it disappeared from sight and the winds picked right back up.

Lightning flashes flickered from within the stormy book, creating monstrous shadows upon the cavern walls. Several seconds later, thunder cracked — miles away in the distance of the book. Roni watched her three teammates for some clue as to what might come next. All three remained stoic as they watched the book. Only the occasional strain against the chains registered on their faces.

Thinking about the chains made Roni aware of the biting sting on her hip. The wind howled as it pulled and pulled. She needed to readjust her chain or soon it would cut into her skin.

With one hand, she slid her fingers along the spine of the chain, seeking the point where it had connected with itself. Hopefully, she could ease it up so she had some room to maneuver. But when she brushed across the connecting end, the clamp sprung open.

She screamed as the wind grabbed hold of her, wrenched her off her feet, and reeled her in toward the book. Her fingers stubbed into the edge of the podium. Panicked, she scrabbled for a grip.

Her legs rose higher, and she heard a shout. "I've got you!" Over her shoulder, she saw Elliot standing with his legs angled and his arm locked around her foot.

She attempted to bend at the waist, to reach out and pull herself closer to Elliot. No good. Her stomach muscles were not strong enough. Something to work on — if she survived this.

A hurricane roar poured out of the book along with a hot, foul odor like a decomposing animal in the worst of summer. With her hands finding holds on the podium, she dared to gaze into the book.

She saw a tunnel of blood-soaked flesh — red and undulating. Like an internal organ exposed to the air, she could see the small veins and arteries along the tunnel walls. Things moved from behind the thin membrane. Some of the things looked like they had faces.

But the tunnel wasn't everything. Roni also saw an opening at the end. Bright light shined and strong winds blew across as if she were in a balloon with miles of sky below. A dark cloud passed by, crackling with lightning, only to be followed by a darker, more violent storm cloud.

As she watched, she felt as if something watched her back. A glance to the side — she saw a human face with jagged teeth and sunken eyes staring at her from behind the membrane. But it vanished, leaving her to question if she had seen it at all.

"Hold on!" Gram yelled.

Roni saw her grandmother whip out a new chain from

her sleeves. This one looked thicker than the others as it flapped in the wind like a streamer. Elliot tried three times to snag it, and on the fourth attempt, he succeeded. He wrapped the chain around Roni's ankle, secured it, and then carefully walked back to the wall, pulling himself along his own chain but never letting go of Roni's chain.

Sully waved his arm in the air and pointed at his watch. "Two minutes left!"

Lowering her head so she wouldn't have to see that horrific tunnel, Roni thought to ask what they would do in two minutes. The thin chains would give way, and she had the distinct impression that the thicker chain keeping her tethered to this world had been an emergency situation. Gram would not be able to create enough of those in time to save the whole team. Making them in the first place must have taken a lot out of her, otherwise, she would have made them all thicker at the start.

Or not. Perhaps she purposely made them thin so that they acted like a timer. Gram had said these other universes brought with them strange bacteria and such. She would want to limit everyone's exposure.

Which meant that if the Golem did not return in time, they would close the book. Darin would be lost forever.

Roni's head snapped towards Gram. She could see it clearly on the old woman's wrinkled face. Gram's lips rolled in as she nodded back. There would be a hard choice coming in less than two minutes. No, not a choice — a duty.

"One minute," Sully called out.

Roni adjusted her grip on the podium and gazed into the book. "Darin!"

"Close the book," Gram said above the harsh winds. "Close it now."

"There's still a minute."

"We can't wait for the chains to snap. Close the book."

Roni strained to see any sign of the Golem or Darin — only sky and the foul tunnel that turned her stomach. She put her hand on the book cover and felt her body pulled closer in. The thick chain on her ankle kept her from spiraling into that blood-drenched abyss.

She saw her hand on the cover. Darin had fallen in there, had seen those faces, and confronted those storms. They couldn't leave him in there. But then they couldn't leave the book open for too much longer. The whole point was to close these rips to protect everyone in the world — not simply one man who lied in order to get to these books.

Gram pointed to Elliot. "Help her."

"I can do it," Roni yelled back.

She tried to lift the cover but the strong winds kept it flat on the podium. Changing her grip, she tried again. Half-an-inch maybe. Putting more muscle into it, she worked to pry the cover loose. A little further. If she could get it to the point that enough air shot underneath, it would snap shut on its own.

But she stopped. A flash of lightning revealed a dark spot in the clouds below. It grew fast as it bulleted toward her.

The Golem!

When it reached the tunnel, its body blocked most of the airway. The winds died and Roni flopped to the ground. She scrambled back to the wall, her heart hammering, her lungs burning.

The chains around her never snapped apart. Instead, they fell to the ground and fractured into hundreds of tiny pieces. Before Roni's astonished eyes, those pieces then broke apart into bits of dust.

Elliot sped across the room with his cane at the ready. The Golem stepped out of the book and the terrible winds returned. But Elliot wedged his cane under the book cover and put his body weight down on the other end. It levered the cover up and over. Before the book had slammed shut, Gram had fresh chains, thick chains wrapping around it.

Roni's shoulders dropped. The Golem had returned empty-handed. "We failed," she said.

"Not at all," Sully said, his eyes on his watch. "4 ... 3 ... 2 ... 1 ..."

The Golem lost all appearance of life. It stood like nothing more than a block of clay. Pieces of it crumbled off. Then more. In seconds, the entire creature disintegrated into a pile of clay pebbles. Standing in the middle of the pile was a naked man. He had stark white hair and his eyes blazed wide open, but Roni knew right away — this was Darin.

CHAPTER 10

For Roni, the next several hours blurred by in a rush of activity. The moment Darin appeared, Elliot jumped into action. Using his cane and hand motions, he checked that Darin was unharmed — physically at least. Sweat poured down Elliot's face as he worked, but when he finally gave Gram an affirmative nod, she said he could rest. Elliot then collapsed.

In a calm yet authoritative voice, Gram instructed Roni to go further into the caverns until she found the door marked with the number 2. Inside, Roni found two wheelchairs. She brought one back and assisted Gram in helping lug Elliot into the chair.

"Get the other one," Gram said.

Roni hustled back to the storage room and wheeled the second chair to the group. She brought it straight to Gram.

"Not for me," Gram said.

Roni looked over at Sully. He had been leaning against the wall ever since the book had been closed. Roni had not given it any thought, but now she saw the pasty look in his face and the stark concentration in his eyes. Sully used all his will to keep standing.

As she helped the man settle in the wheelchair, she thought how frail these people really were. They could summon tremendous strength in short bursts but nothing could change the fact that their bodies had been around a long time. Sixties and seventies were not ages for most people to be fighting off other universes.

"They'll be fine," Gram said, as if she could read Roni's mind. "A good night's sleep and they'll be back up as if nothing ever happened."

Roni imagined a porcupine in a tutu and then stared hard at Gram. After a moment, Gram raised her eyebrows. "What?"

"Nothing," Roni said, hiding her relief. "Just testing something."

"I can't read minds."

"How do you know that's what I —"

"I've known you for your entire life. I can read your face easy."

Roni decided to accept the explanation. "Are you sure you don't need help, too?" she asked.

"Elliot healed me right before we started this. I'm fine. Another time might be different."

Following more orders, Roni wheeled each man to the elevator and took them to their apartment while Gram kept on eye on Darin. For his part, Darin never moved. He barely blinked. He stared straight ahead, and never even flinched when Gram placed a robe from the storage room around his body. Even though it appeared that Darin would be no trouble, Roni hurried to situate Elliot and Sully so that she could return to the caverns as fast as possible.

When she finally rejoined Gram, part of her wished she had stayed with Sully. She had heard of the soldier's thousand yard stare, and she had seen the glazed look of dementia patients. Put the two together and it came close to what she saw in Darin's eyes — close but not enough.

"What do we do now?" Roni asked.

Gram looked him over. "He's alive, and Elliot said he's in good enough health. We'll cut him loose. Let him decide for himself what he does now."

"We can't do that."

"What do you think we should do? Hold him prisoner against his will?"

"First off, look at him. He looks out of his mind. And after what he just saw, he probably is lucky for that. Don't we have a responsibility to him?"

"We didn't ask him to break into our private rooms and attempt to steal from us. He did this to himself."

"But what if he talks to people? He's seen what you can do."

Gram rubbed the back of her hands as she flexed her fingers. "I swear, these old hands get worse every day."

"Gram!"

"Stop worrying. You think this has never happened before? That in centuries of these books being in existence, you think nobody has ever discovered the secret we hold? Nothing will happen. We let him go, and he'll return to his life. Or he won't. That's his business. If he tells anybody what he saw, where he was, any of it at all, you know what will happen?"

Roni knew right away. "They'll think he's crazy."

"If he's lucky, they'll think he's joking or having a bad day or something like that. If he's unlucky, he'll be institutionalized in a psychiatric facility, possibly for the rest of his life. Which, I'll point out, is not always the worst outcome. Considering what happened to him, a shrink could be exactly what he'll need."

Crossing her arms, Roni bumped her back against the

wall. She swallowed down the bubble of emotion riding up her throat. Her voice shook as she said, "Dad is institutionalized."

"Exactly. You know that he gets good care. If Darin's mind can't handle what he saw, he can get good care, too."

"I-Is that what happened to Dad? Did he see into another universe?"

Gram's face shifted as she put out her arms. "Honey, no. Your father never knew about this side of our life. He simply loved your mother — more than most ever love another. When she died, he couldn't take it. That's all. I promise."

She hugged Roni, and for a few seconds, being smothered by Gram's large bosom felt safe. But then Roni lifted her head and saw Darin.

"Doesn't this trouble you?"

Following Roni's gaze, Gram stepped back and straightened her robe. "I'm too old to worry about things that don't matter. He'll fall into whatever he falls into. Serves him right for meddling where he doesn't belong."

"That part, though. That's what I mean. Shouldn't we be concerned about the fact that he must be working for somebody. He obviously used a date with me as a way to gain access to the caverns. That means he targeted me specifically. I saw where he works, and I met his mother. Trust me. This man is not a criminal mastermind, and I didn't see anything to indicate that he would be taking the time to watch me, learn my habits, confirm that I'd be able to get him into the basement, and then try to charm me into a date so he could steal a book all on his own. Not this man."

"I'll think on it, but you need to get used to it. A secret as big as ours is never really a secret. He wouldn't be the first to attempt to steal a book for somebody else. As long as there have been people like us fighting to protect our universe, there also have been those who want access to these other worlds. For greed, for power, for curiosity, in some cases for religious confirmation — whatever the reason, you'll learn that sometimes our worst fights are with other people, not the creatures living in these universes."

"I suppose," Roni said. Then her head caught up. "Did you say creatures?"

Gram smirked. "We'll deal with that another time. Please escort Darin out onto the street. He's not to be our problem anymore."

Roni knew Gram's tones well — the conversation was over. Without another word, Roni took Darin by the hand and walked back up through the cavern. He followed simply and quietly. Even his footsteps were quiet.

In the elevator, she watched his immobile face. Nothing. He stared blankly at the wall. More than anything, his white hair spoke volumes of the horror he had witnessed. And not just the hair on his head. His eyebrows, his whiskers, even the hair on his arms — all of it had gone stark white.

On the main floor, she led him out the front door. The sun rose to start a new day. How could that be possible? Roni had no idea so many hours had gone by. She felt tired but not the *up all night* tired she knew from her college days. In that cavern, there were no natural indicators of the passage of time, and so much had happened that she never bothered to check her phone. But an entire night?

She would have to ask Gram or the boys about that. For now, though, she had to deal with Darin. He stood on the sidewalk, his eyes roving up and down the street. That seemed like an improvement.

"Darin? Can you hear me?"

He turned his head towards her.

"Hi," she said. "You're safe now. We got you back."

He said nothing. He only gazed upon her face with an inscrutable expression.

"That's okay," she said. "I'm guessing it'll take a while for you to readjust."

She thought about what Gram had said — that she should let Darin loose to find his own way, that he would probably end up committed to a mental hospital of some kind, and that he would be better off there because professionals could look after him. Except she couldn't do that. Maybe an institution was where he would end up, but she had to give him a chance for something better, at least.

"Come on with me," she said. Leading him by the hand, she walked to her car. They got in — she had to buckle his seatbelt for him — and she headed west for Lancaster. "I'm taking you home."

CHAPTER 11

As she drove west on Route 30, Roni discovered that some lies are easier than others. For the entire length of the trip, she struggled to come up with any story that would be plausible. One look at Darin, and his mother would know something serious had happened. On top of which, Roni had to maintain the fiction that she was Darin's girlfriend.

She texted Jane to let her know she was coming and that she had Darin. Roni figured this would put Jane in a joyous mood, and that might ease down whatever lie she could concoct. When she pulled up to the house, Jane rushed across the front lawn, tears streaming, arms open.

After kisses upon kisses, shock at his appearance and tears at his arrival, Darin's mother helped him into the house. Roni followed, still unsure of what to say, but Jane didn't ask. She focused entirely on her son. With a hug, a kiss, a hand always on him as if afraid he might vanish, Jane brought him upstairs to his childhood bedroom, now a plain guest room.

From the doorway, Roni watched as Jane clucked about the room. She chatted to Darin about her worries and fears and the neighborhood gossip and anything else that came to mind. All the while, she wiped down the dresser, fluffed the pillows, and cleared away some toys for a cat Roni had yet to see.

Darin stood in the center of the room, staring out the window. At one point, Jane halted her manic preparations and put her hand on his cheek. He tilted his head towards her — just a bit — and his lips formed a hint of a smile.

"You probably need a little rest. We'll let you be. Okay? We can talk at dinner." She kissed him again and shooed Roni downstairs.

When they entered the living room, Roni headed for the couch, but Jane pointed down the hall. She followed Darin's mother through the kitchen and into a back room. It was small and lacked all the charm the rest of the house held. An ironing board stood against one wall. Two folding chairs had been placed next to a window, and an ashtray sat on one chair next to a pack of cigarettes.

Jane lifted the window open and set the ashtray on the ledge. She sat in one chair, pulled out a lighter from her pocket, and grabbed the cigarettes. As she lit up, she indicated the now empty chair for Roni. Though Roni did not smoke, she noticed that Jane never offered her a cigarette.

Puffing away, Jane stared out the window. Roni started to speak, but Jane put out her hand. They remained quiet until she had smoked half of her cigarette.

"I'm sure you have quite a story to tell me, but I don't want to hear it."

"I know you think —"

"Don't embarrass yourself. Be smart and shut up."

Roni didn't know whether to be happy or concerned — especially because she never did come up with a good explanation.

Jane went on, "I really thought we had hit it off. I

suppose on some level you were being honest with me. But I don't want to listen to you lie about Darin. It's obvious that you knew where he was and what he was up to when you came here. You must have at least had an idea of where he could be. Otherwise, you never would have been able to bring him back so soon. Then again, you didn't really bring him back, did you? You brought me a ghost of my son. So, if you ever gave a crap about him, if anything you told me was true, then please answer me directly. Is he a drug addict now? Did you get him hooked on something that made him this way?"

"No. Never." Roni did not have to pretend her shock.

"Do you know what's wrong with him?"

She hesitated, and Jane picked up on it right away.

"You won't tell me, will you?"

"I'm sorry," Roni said. "I really can't. It wouldn't matter anyway."

"How can you say that? You've seen him. He looks older than me. What did you do to him that would cause that?"

"I didn't do anything. I swear. He did it to himself."

"What?"

"He ... well, it's like he stuck his hand in a raging fire and then was surprised that he got burned."

Jane stubbed out her cigarette with more force than necessary. "You're blaming him for this?"

"It's not like that. It's hard to explain. I mean, I can't explain it. I'm not allowed to." Roni dropped her head into her hands. "I'm messing this whole thing up."

"That's evident. Why don't you stop tiptoeing around the things you can't tell me, and start with the things you can tell me? How about that?"

Roni thought it over a moment. Crafting her words carefully, she said, "Your son asked me out on a date because he needed access to where I work. I didn't know that at the time. I thought he liked me. But he didn't care about me at all. He used me to get into a private collection of items and exposed himself to highly dangerous, um, things. It was contact with those things that changed him."

"And I take it you won't ever tell me what those things are."

"I can't. I don't even know for sure what he saw or exactly how it all happened for him. But I do know that you shouldn't treat him like he's crazy. You'd be better off approaching him as if he were a war veteran or something — a person with PTSD. That might get you the best results."

Jane digested this information before leveling her coldest glare at Roni. "I want you to leave my house and never come back. I don't ever want to see you again. If, someday years from now, you walk into a store or a restaurant or anywhere, and you see me, please have the decency to leave so that I don't have to endure the pain of being reminded you exist."

Roni wanted to say something that would repair the damage, but those cold eyes stopped her. Unlike Darin's lifeless eyes, Jane's spewed an icy venom that threatened violence along with the hatred behind them. Roni lowered her gaze as she stood.

"I am sorry," she said. "I had no idea that Darin had intended —"

"Get out!" Jane's body quaked as she yelled.

Roni left. She got back in her car and turned the key. Nothing happened. She tried again and heard a slight whine. She could feel Darin's mother watching from the living room window. Trying again, she almost had it. Ten more excruciating seconds went by before the engine finally turned over.

She floored the gas and screeched her tires as she roared onto the street. As fast as the road would allow her, she got onto the highway and made for home. But in Lancaster, Route 30 had sections which could slow down to a baby crawl — especially around the shopping outlets. After twenty minutes and four lights — miles of store after store after store — she needed a break.

When she hit the small village of Ronks, she knew she had finally gone through the last major section of shopping outlets. On her left, she saw Miller's Smorgasbord — a Pennsylvania Dutch all-you-can-eat buffet that had been in Lancaster for decades. That sounded perfect.

In minutes, she had parked, entered, grabbed a plate, and piled on the food. Mashed potatoes, macaroni and cheese, and dried corn. A chef standing by a slab of roast beef cut her three lovely slices to which she added a thick gravy. She set the plate at her table and returned to make a second plate with a baked potato, creamed spinach, and popcorn shrimp. On her way back, she saw a slice of shoofly pie which she nabbed with her free hand.

Sitting in the back corner, she stared at her gluttonous banquet and felt all desire to eat drain from her gut. All the food slapped together on her plates reminded her of the twisted mess she had seen within that book. A tunnel of evil stretching down to a tumultuous sky. But at times it became a pleasant sky. It could not have been too pleasant — it destroyed Darin's mind.

All for what? Even if he had succeeded, what then? After such an experience, would he simply hand the book over to whomever had hired him? Just take the money and forget about it?

No. He would never be able to do that. Unless they were paying an enormous sum. Which, considering the value of a book like that, they just might.

Since Darin would not be delivering the book, the buyers would most likely be sending others to steal it. The more she thought about it, the more she understood why Darin chose to go through her. Gram was too old to play at a date, and all three of the Old Gang had been defending their turf for so long that they would have recognized Darin for what he was right away. Which meant that the others who might come looking for the books would also attempt to get it through Roni.

I'm never going to be to able date again, she thought with a chuckle. But the humor faded fast. Not only would she forever have to doubt the motivations of those she came into contact with, but she could never warn them either. After all, she would not know who was an authentic person and who was a liar attempting to steal a book until that person took action. After that point, it would be too late — as it was too late to save Darin.

She hated the thought that crept beneath the surface, the thought that she knew she had been circling for too long, the thought she feared giving voice to — but the time had arrived. Staring at all her untouched food, she said, "I can't be a part of this."

Usually, when she voiced a decision that troubled her, she felt better. Not this time. Because voicing it did not put it into action nor did it make the next step any easier. She had to tell Gram.

The lengthy drive back to Olburg mounted the dread for her. She envisioned the arguments Gram would make, the anger and fierce words Gram might throw at her, and she prepared her counter-arguments. But in the end, she knew how it would stand — she had agreed to join the group, and only a day or so later, she was backing out. It didn't help that Gram, Elliot, and Sully were approaching the ends of their lives. At least, that was what Gram would say. The fact that they had at least a decade each to go meant nothing to them — especially considering the dangerous lifestyle they lived.

Back and forth the debate raged in Roni's head until she blared rock music to drown out her thoughts. It worked for a short time. Nothing, however, could stop the inevitable. Roni reached the bookstore.

The front door was locked. Gram had mentioned that she would not open the store for the day — Elliot and Sully needed rest. Roni used her key to get in, locked the door behind her, and rode the elevator to the top floor. She knocked on Gram's door.

"Come in," Gram called from her kitchen.

Roni entered the comfortable apartment. Decorated with the right balance of furniture, rugs, books, and paintings to create a cozy, lived-in feel, the rooms never bordered on cluttered or dirty. In the kitchen, Roni found Gram sitting at a small, round table eating her lunch — a tuna sandwich with a dill pickle on the side.

Gram's welcoming smile faded when she saw Roni. "What's wrong?"

Standing in the doorway, Roni picked at her nails, keeping her eyes down, and figured barreling through would be her best option. "No easy way to say any of this, but after looking into that book and seeing what it did to Darin and then I thought about the years ahead, well —"

"It's not usually like this. If it was, we never would have lived this long."

"Still, I don't think this is right for me."

"I see." Gram returned to her sandwich.

"I want to help you, but I don't see how I can go through what you all do. Especially because you have powers. I'm just a regular person."

"Sure. We'll find somebody else to take your place." She

gazed out the window near the kitchen table.

Roni's fingers clenched. "Don't be like that."

"What now?" Gram said, still remaining calm. "You said you don't want to be in this, and I said that was fine. What's the matter? You want out, you got out."

"Don't you even care? Or am I just another employee?"

"I learned long ago that I can't force you to do the right thing. I never could."

"And there it is," Roni said like a lawyer who caught a witness in a lie. "You think what I'm doing is wrong. You always think I make the wrong choice."

"No, Roni. You are the one who thinks you make the wrong choice. But then you do it anyway. The fact is that I told you to walk away from all of this before you learned too much. Now that you know, you regret getting involved. Well, I'm sorry that reality isn't filled with all the easy-living dreams you wanted, but that's reality no matter what universe you're in. Running away from your commitments won't change that. I would have thought you'd have figured that out by now."

"Are you saying that I run from commitment?"

Gram set her sandwich down and wiped her mouth with a napkin. "You clearly want to have a fight, so I'll ask you to leave. I'd like to eat in peace. Also, please leave your key to the store by the register."

Roni's face dropped. "You're kicking me out? Firing me?"

"You were never hired, so I can't really fire you."

"But I'm no longer welcome here — is that it?"

Gram leaned back in her chair. As she played with the beads on her necklace, her stern face grew dark. "We shared with you our greatest secrets, and we did so because you made a commitment to us. These secrets take precedence over all else in our lives — even family. I love you, Roni. I truly do. I don't regret all the years spent raising you after your mother died. I don't want you thinking that. But if you are not part of this group, then you cannot be in this building ever again. The secrets we hold here are too important, too powerful, for us to risk another Darin situation."

Roni wanted to scream. But she wanted to break down crying, too. Before her body or mind could decide which reaction to have, her cellphone rang. Out of habit, she glanced at the screen — Jane Lander.

Roni accepted the call. "Jane?"

"You have to come back here right now. You just have to. I don't know what to do. What's going on with him? I need your help."

"Calm down. What's happened?"

"It's Darin. He's gone."

CHAPTER 12

Roni ignored the sickening roil in her stomach as she drove yet again to Lancaster. Part of her felt ill over what might have happened to Darin. But mostly, she felt ill over Gram.

Their argument — and no matter how pleasant a face Gram put on it, Roni knew it was an argument — had not ended with Jane Lander's phone call. If anything, it grew worse.

"I'm on my way," Roni had said to Jane.

But after ending the call, Gram said, "You most certainly are not. This is a situation that no longer has anything to do with you."

"How can you say that?"

"I didn't. You're the one who wanted to quit all of this. Well then, quit. Elliot, Sully, and I have been dealing with jokers like Darin for ages. We'll find him, and we'll take care of it."

"And what's that mean? You'll lock him away in a mental hospital? Or maybe you'll drive him out to Philly or Baltimore and let him loose to live out his life as another homeless person talking to himself on the street corner. Is that your idea of taking care of it?"

"You think I would do that after —"

"You told me to do that very thing. Why wouldn't I expect you to do it, too?"

"Because, young lady," Gram said, her glower silencing Roni, "things changed when you brought him to his mother's house. You've involved other people, extra variables, and so the simple option, the one I suggested for you, no longer applies."

"But —"

"You can argue all day long but it won't change the truth. And while you're waffling on where you actually stand in these matters, remember that Darin is out there, walking around. The longer we wait to find him, the more likely our chance that something bad will happen. So, make up your mind. Are you part of this team or not?"

Roni's eyes narrowed. She felt her pulse beating along her neck and up the side of her head. "I'm going out to find him."

Gram's mouth raised into an annoying *knowing* smile. "Then we're glad to have you stay with us."

"Only for this job. Once all of this with Darin is sorted out, I'm done."

Roni didn't wait to hear or see Gram's reaction. She stormed out of the apartment and took the stairs down to her car. That was over an hour ago.

As she neared Lancaster, Roni cleared her mind of her personal problems and focused on finding Darin. Thankfully, Darin's mother had the sense to keep this private. Had she called the police, and if they found him, he would certainly be held for psychiatric assessment. This way, at least, they could bring Darin back to Jane's house.

But was that even the best thing to do for him? Roni had no idea how to gauge such a determination when dealing with other universes, hellish tunnels, and magic warriors. She let free a short laugh at the idea of Gram and her boys as magic warriors.

In the town of Gap, there was one intersection with a traffic light at the bottom of a steep hill. Slowing down for the red light, Roni's jaw dropped. There he was. Walking on the side of the road and headed her way. She pulled into the parking lot for a local chain of pizza shops called Two Cousins and got out.

"Darin! Are you okay?"

Approaching him with caution, she marveled at her luck in stumbling upon him. But then she decided it hadn't been luck at all. Route 30 was the main road connecting Lancaster with Philadelphia. Presumably, Darin wanted to get back to his own home or perhaps his office at Page Brothers. It wasn't strange at all, then, that he would take this route. But walking? That was strange.

She stepped in front of him and he stopped. "Hi, there. Remember me? Roni?"

"I need to get to the zoo."

"The Philadelphia Zoo? That's a long way from here." She pointed toward the pizza shop. "You'll need your energy, and I'm starving. Missed out on lunch. Let's go sit and have a bite. We'll figure out how to get you to the zoo. Sound good?"

She didn't wait for an answer. Taking him by the arm, she led him into the restaurant. He did not resist.

The savory aroma of cheesesteaks and pizza caused her stomach to growl. At the counter, she ordered two cheesesteaks — one with mushrooms and one with sweet peppers. On their date the night before, Darin had mentioned liking sweet peppers. At least, she thought he did.

They sat in a booth — the place was empty — and while they waited for the food, she rifled off a text to Jane telling her that Darin was safe and would be home soon. She also texted Gram saying much the same. Then she set the phone down and took hold of his hands.

"You in there? Remember this? You and me out on a date? This is how it all started. I know you used me to get to the books, but maybe you actually enjoyed our date a little. See, I'm thinking that you're like a coma patient, and if I keep connecting you with the real world, if you keep hearing my voice and remembering our date, then maybe you'll come back."

"I'm here," he said in a monotone. "I need to go to the zoo."

A man walked out with their food. He set down two plates and two plastic, red baskets that each had a cheesesteak. After he returned to the kitchen, Roni jumped right in, taking a big bite of her sandwich.

"I need to go to the zoo."

"I know," she said around a mouthful of food. "I'll figure out how to get you there, but right now, you should eat. You've got to understand that your mother is worried about you. And there are others, too. People who want to make sure you don't cause any trouble about the books. So, let's eat up, and I'll take you home. Then we can work on getting you to the zoo, if that's what you want."

She nudged his plate closer. He glanced down, and something must have clicked in his head because he picked up his food and took a bite. And another. He pushed the food in fast, chewing hard, as he tried to inhale the whole thing.

"Slow down. You'll choke."

But he continued to wolf down each bite. "Good," he grunted.

"Darin, I want you to listen to me. Can you do that?"

He stopped eating and raised his head.

"I want to help you," she said, putting her hand on the table, palm up. "I forgive you for using our date to get to the caverns. I don't know why you did it or if somebody hired you or what, but I forgive you. Nobody deserves what happened to you. But in order for me to help, I have to understand what exactly happened. What did you see in there that scared you so much?"

Darin scanned the room, but Roni could not tell if he searched for an attack or an escape. "I need to get to the zoo."

"Why the zoo? What's there? What's so important?"

He reached across the table and clasped both hands to her face. "You want to help me? Zoo." Before she could answer, he leaned closer and kissed her on the lips.

When he returned to his seat, he tucked into the remainder of his meal. Roni watched him, the taste of him lingering on her lips — sweet and clean. He peeked up at her like a schoolboy afraid he had scared off the girl. But then a mature look crossed his face, one filled with masculine confidence.

He leaned back and grinned. "Don't take me back to Lancaster. I love my mother, but she can't handle this right now. I'll be better off at my apartment. Can we go there?"

Roni could not move. She could not speak. Her brain kept trying to process that this man who had been like a zombie suddenly spoke free and fluent while flirting with her in a casual manner. She had no idea what to make of any of it, but she agreed with one thing — taking him back to his mother's place would be a bad idea.

"Sure," she finally said. "Let's go to your apartment. We'll figure things out from there."

After clearing their trash and placing the red baskets on the counter, they got in Roni's car and drove toward the Philly area. Darin moved like a normal person — strolling to the car, settling in the passenger seat, buckling up. It was as if some loose wires had reconnected and his brain now worked properly.

Except Roni did not feel comfortable. A voice deep within urged her to drop Darin off at his apartment, get the heck out of there, go to the bookstore, and report everything to Gram.

No. That was her nerves talking. Too many cop shows and horror movies had warped her sense of human behavior. Not to mention the fact that Darin's behavior could not be predicted upon anything she had ever experienced. She had no base for measuring how a man would react to being pulled into a book and seeing insane things only to be rescued by a clay statue come to life.

Darin lived about ten minutes from his law office. His apartment building stood two blocks off the main drag next to a small park that consisted mostly of a basketball court and a thin patch of grass. Roni parked on the street, and they walked up together.

He lived on the third floor, and from what Roni could see, the place desperately needed to be remodeled. Probably hadn't had any major work since the 1960s.

The apartment itself looked much better. When it came to cleanliness and organization, Darin had followed in his mother's footsteps. Even after a few days of neglect, the place sparkled. Not a fleck of dust had dared to settle on the carefully positioned furniture.

"Damn," Roni said. "This place even smells perfect."

"Wait here." Darin set his keys on a silver plate by the door and disappeared down the single hallway that led to a bathroom and a bedroom.

"Sure. No problem." She pulled out her phone and rang up Jane. "I found him."

Jane cried for a moment and reduced it to a few sniffles.

"Thank goodness," she said. "Tell me where you are and I'll come pick him up."

"That's not necessary. He asked me to take him back to his apartment. I don't know what happened to him, but he's starting to sound normal again."

"Don't be foolish. He obviously needs my care right now. Unless you're planning on spending the next few days with him until we know for sure that he's okay. I take it by your silence that you won't be doing that. So, please, get in your car and drive him back."

"I can't. He specifically asked to be here, and I'm inclined to —"

"I don't care about your inclinations. I want my son home, in my house, by the end of the day."

Back in her high school days, Roni had crossed swords with more than her share of overprotective parents. The psychologist Gram had her seeing once said that losing her parents at such a young age had created a void, and she sought to fill that void with boyfriends. Maybe. But maybe it had more to do with the type of boyfriend she chose rather than choosing any boy. As an adult, however, Roni had no intention of letting another parent walk all over her — even if she wasn't really Darin's girlfriend to begin with.

"No," Roni said. "I am not driving between Philly and Lancaster again. Not tonight. Darin told me he wanted to be in his own place and that's where he is. You want to dote on him? Be my guest. Come on by tomorrow at any time, and he's all yours."

"Now you listen to me."

"Jane. I called you so that you wouldn't worry about your son, not so that you could yell at me. Good night." Before Jane could say another word, Roni ended the call.

"Thank you," Darin said from the hallway. He walked out of the shadows wearing his pajama bottoms and a t-shirt. "I love her. I do. But I have important things to do, and she would only get in my way."

Roni plopped down on the couch. "You don't have to do anything tonight. Come here. Sit."

Darin obliged, settling in next to her. She put her arm around his shoulders as he nestled his head on her chest. "I have to get to a zoo."

"Tomorrow. You can explain it all to me then. I'm just glad you're okay. You are, right?"

He peeked up at her. "I don't know what I am."

Stroking his hair, she said, "Of course. You've been through a lot. We all have."

"The zoo," he said, but his words drifted off.

Roni let her head fall to the back of the couch. She closed her eyes. Nothing felt right in this apartment, but she was too tired to do anything about it. Besides, she needed to stay for Darin. Tomorrow, Jane would come and Roni could be done with it. Until then, she would have to take care of him.

Darin's soft snoring drifted up to her ears. "Well," she whispered, "at least one of us can get some rest. I don't think I'll be sleeping for a long time. How'd I even get here? Not your apartment but here — this moment. I'll tell you, the last forty-eight hours have been so insane — just one thing after another that took all I knew and turned it into mush. I don't know what to make of it. I haven't had time. Now that I'm here, all I want to do is sleep and my brain won't shut up.

"I mean, take yourself. Here you are, lying to me from the beginning — I should be so angry at you. I shouldn't care at all what happens to you. Yet all I want to do is heal you, fix you. And not in some childish, schoolgirl way of 'Oh, my. He's a broken man, and I'm the only one who can fix him.' No. I feel responsible. Like maybe if I had refused to let you go down in that basement, if I had not simply shown it to you. I know you probably would have found some other way down there, but at least then, it wouldn't be weighing on my shoulders.

"And then — pay attention here because this is something that I keep dwelling on — if I hadn't brought you straight to that basement, if you had been forced to find a different way in, then I wouldn't have had to be part of saving you. I wouldn't have learned anything about any of it. You would have been nothing more to me than some guy who dated me once and never called me again. That would have been much easier.

"Now, what do I do? I can't really go back to a normal life after all of this. I don't see how I could ever pretend none of this has happened. But I've screwed everything up with Gram. She's been so good to me over the years. Yes, she lied to me, too — I haven't forgotten. But I get it. She couldn't tell me the truth. Look how I'm handling it now. I can't imagine how I would have handled it any earlier in my life.

"I just wish there was some way I could get all this set right. Some way to not have you screwed up in the head and not have Gram mad at me."

Roni chuckled. "Strangest thing. I think even if I could fix everything else, I wouldn't want to go back to not knowing the truth. I mean, it sucks knowing — not being able to tell anybody. It sucks thinking how twisted and bizarre the universe is and how at any moment, if the Old Gang fails at their job, all of our existence might get ruined forever. But at the same time, I kind of like knowing. I like that our world is truly magic. I mean there's real magic out there. It gives me a perspective that feels right."

Crossing her feet on the glass coffee table, knowing she would leave behind a smudge, she said, "Who am I kidding? It's all screwed up. It'll always be screwed up. That's the way life is. We keep thinking we can control it, fix it, bring order to it, but chaos is the natural state of things." She glanced down at the snowy hair. "At least tomorrow I can put you right. I know it can't go back exactly the way it was — hair color ain't changing for one thing — but we'll get you some help. Maybe a psychiatrist. Something. Then this job will be done, and I guess I'll have to find a new job somewhere."

Roni rambled on for a few more minutes and never realized when she fell asleep.

CHAPTER 13

Roni's eyes did not want to open. She could have used another hour of sleep — maybe two — but as she rubbed an itch out of her nose, she knew sleep would not return for the day. The stiffness in her back and the crick in her neck attested that she had fallen asleep sitting up. But she felt no weight on her chest. Her eyes snapped open.

Where was Darin?

She zipped down the hall and poked her head in his bedroom. Empty. The bed looked like a model display at a linen store. Nobody had slept here.

"Dar —" she tried to call out but her voice cracked under the strain. She tended to hold tension in her neck, so whenever she held a lot of tension for too long — such as sleeping tense for a few hours — losing her voice often followed. Though inconvenient, she had been through it many times before. If she took care not to talk too much, her voice would return later in the day. Of course, getting rid of the tension would be most helpful, but she did not see that happening anytime soon — especially if she couldn't find Darin.

She walked back up the hall and stopped to check in the

bathroom. Empty. And clean and well-appointed.

Back in the living room, she glimpsed the balcony. A terrible thought jumped into her head and she darted to the railing. Gazing over the ledge, she searched the sidewalk below — no blood, no corpse, nothing. Thank goodness. She would rather have been waterboarded than have to tell Jane Lander that her son had committed suicide.

Inside, she crossed the living room and entered the kitchen. Bingo. Darin stood in the center of the functional but minuscule kitchen. Slack-jawed and leaning over like a man determined to spend his later years hunched over with pain in his back, Darin faced a framed, artistic print of lions walking across an open plain. She guessed the Serengeti. He did not appear to notice anything around him.

Careful not to jar him or make any sudden loud noises, Roni stepped over to the refrigerator and poured herself a glass of orange juice. Then she inched into Darin's field of vision, closed her eyes against the expectation of pain, and said, "Darin? Can you hear me?"

The words scratched her throat, but they came out clear and audible. She opened her eyes. Darin showed no reaction.

In the living room, Roni dug through her purse until she found her cellphone. She brought up Gram's number, but her thumb hovered over the call button. Things were bad enough. Roni didn't want to make it all worse and give Gram even more reasons to be against her.

Instead, she called Sully. He had made the Golem statue and Darin acted like a statue. Granted, the tenuous connection offered nothing to be hopeful about, but when she listened to the phone ring, hope sparked in her nonetheless. But Sully did not answer.

Perhaps Elliot's healing ability would solve the problem. She called him, though no hope grew within her. After all, if Elliot had the power to heal whatever problem Darin had, surely he would have done so the moment Darin had returned from the book. The call went straight to voicemail.

Roni bumped the heel of her hand against the side of her head. Foolish. Sully and Elliot still recuperated from their ordeal. They wouldn't be answering phone calls. She would have to drive out there and see them in person.

Gathering her things together, she wondered if Darin would be safe alone. Probably. In all likelihood, he would remain in the kitchen staring at the wall. Plus, she could be at *In The Bind* within twenty minutes, if she hit the traffic lights right. Thirty minutes, otherwise. A few words with Sully, and they would return. Less than an hour gone.

Convinced Darin would be fine, Roni sped down the stairwell, out onto the street, and into her car. Luck graced her with no traffic, no police, and all green lights. Seventeen minutes and twelve seconds later, she parked and walked up to the bookstore.

The front door had been set open which meant, at the least, Gram minded the store. It also meant that the electronic bell would be turned on. It rang a simple two-tone chime whenever somebody crossed the entranceway to alert Gram of a customer. If Roni intended to get to Sully and Elliot without encountering Gram — which she very much did — she had to wait.

Luck stayed with her — a young couple with a baby in a stroller approached the store. Roni didn't want to consider how much good luck she had wasted on this trip already, and instead, she hoped it would last a bit longer. Staying close behind the couple, she walked into the store, letting the electronic bell ring out. Right away, she spotted Gram with another customer off to the left. Roni headed to the right and behind the first aisle of books.

"Welcome to *In The Bind*," Gram said. "Browsing or can

I help you find something?"

"We're looking for a gift for a friend. He's big into old histories and that kind of thing."

"Come with me. I'll show you what we have."

The History section put Gram's trajectory directly in Roni's path. No problem, though. Roni grew up in this bookstore. Years of playing hide-n-seek would finally pay off — though, Roni had to admit that this particular round brought with it no sense of fun or play.

As Gram led the couple deeper into the store, Roni crouched behind a short shelf, and crossed to the left. She scurried to the end of the aisle and swiftly maneuvered her way to the back wall. Here she had to wait until Gram finished with the couple — the stairs and the elevator were both within easy sight lines of the History section.

Sitting on the floor, waiting, she remembered those years when playing like this would have been the height of fun. A miserable cloud followed her actions now — not just this day, with all the pressures of her recent awakening to reality, but most days. As a child, despite the tragedy of losing her parents, she had mostly happy memories.

Those that lasted. She had only a few.

At length, Roni heard Gram say what she had waited for — "I'll take this up front and when you're ready, it'll be waiting for you." She counted to ten, giving Gram enough time to walk away but not enough time to reach the counter. With Gram's back to the stairs, Roni had a clear shot and she took it.

As fast and as silent as possible, she slipped across the aisles and up the stairs to the second floor. From there, she could relax as she traversed flight after flight until she reached the fifth floor. Elliot's door had been propped open — he claimed to prefer the air circulation but Roni always suspected Elliot preferred being able to see who came and went.

She entered the apartment, rapping her knuckles on the door. "Hello? Elliot? Sully?"

"Back here," Elliot called out.

Roni found both men sitting at the small kitchen table, each one concentrating hard on the cards fanned in their hands. "Good morning."

"Uh-oh," Sully said. "Your voice is all broken up. Rough night?"

Elliot tapped Sully's arm. "Do you recall the time when she went on one of her first dates. A boy she really liked a lot and after waiting all day, she could barely talk."

"Or the time she had to get up in front of the school and —"

"Okay, enough," Roni said. "We all know that this happens to me. Not as often as it did, though. Keep that in mind."

"Always," Elliot said with a smirk.

"What are you playing?"

"Just some Gin," Sully said. "And I'm not doing so well."

Elliot pushed out a chair. "Care to join us?"

Both men wore their bedclothes beneath full-length robes. A glance downward revealed slippers on their feet. Sully caught her gaze. "Don't worry about us. We're feeling a million times better."

"You've got Elliot here to take care of you, right?"

"As much as possible," Elliot said.

Sully coughed — a hard, phlegm-filled sound that did not encourage the image of health. "What brings you up here?"

Elliot laid down his cards. "Gin."

"Damn." Sully tossed his cards on the table and pushed his glasses up his nose. "Not that we aren't happy to see you for just a visit. Frankly, after your spat with your grandmother, I was afraid we might not get to see you for a long time. But here you are."

"Here I am," she said as she sat. "I doubt Gram would greet me with half the joy you fellows show me."

Elliot shuffled the cards. "Oh, don't look at it like that. Your grandmother is rough, you know that, but she's good-hearted, too."

"I know, but —"

"Let an old man speak. You might learn something. She has been through a lot."

Sully snorted. "We all have."

"Yeah, but she was doing this job long before us. She's seen more. And fighting with you is not what she wants. But she loves this job. She loves it, respects it, and values it above all else. It's not personal."

"Of course, it is." Roni crossed her arms. She caught her reflection in the glass of a photograph on the wall and saw a young version of Gram. Snapping her arms to her sides, she said, "I know you two have worked with her a long time, but remember that I'm no stranger here. I've known her my whole life. For her, everything is personal."

With a begrudging nod, Elliot said, "All I'm trying to say is that when you agreed to join us and then changed your mind so fast, you sort of bruised the thing she holds most important. Understand?"

Sully said, "And I'm old, but not a fool. You're not here on a social visit and you didn't come for family relationship advice. What do you need?"

Roni checked her watch. She already had spent too much time trying to get up to the apartment and now wished she had taken the time and effort to have brought Darin along. But then Darin would be outside, sitting in a hot car — she couldn't very well bring him inside with

Gram running the store — and the chances of things getting worse would have grown exponentially. No, she had made the right choice. But getting back to him fast also needed to happen.

She launched into an abbreviated version of events culminating in Darin's current state and her lack of solutions. When she finished, she said, "I thought that maybe you'd be willing to come out to Darin's place and take a look at him. Maybe you could help."

The men shared a mischievous twinkle. Sully then said, "I assume you don't want your grandmother to know about this."

"That might be best for now."

Elliot chuckled. "We'll absolutely help you."

From a sideways glance, Roni said, "Why are you happy to do this behind Gram's back?"

"Number one — we want to help you. Truly. Number two — it's fun to do stuff in secret. That's part of the allure of this job."

Tapping his nose and pointing, Sully said, "Plus, at our age, any secretive fun that's new is extra fun, and we want as much of that as we can get. We never know when our last day is coming, and I can't expect Elliot to save me all the time."

Checking her watch again, Roni said, "Fine, fine. But we need to go now. You boys take the elevator down and meet me out by my car. I'll take the stairs and go out the back. If you run into Gram, stall her a little, please."

Elliot rubbed his hands and laughed. "This is getting better every minute. Let's go."

CHAPTER 14

When they approached the door to Darin's apartment, Roni's heart sank. It stood halfway ajar. Her lips rolled in as she fought back the urge to scream.

Like a newfound mantra, she said, "No, no, no, no, no."

She bolted into the apartment, racing down the hall to check the bedroom, slamming open the bathroom door, and ending with the room she knew she would not find him — the kitchen.

"He's gone." Her voice was a mouse peep almost drowned out by the rattling air conditioner.

"Don't worry about it," Sully said. "Do you know how many times we've botched up a job? Goes with the territory. I mean, the learning curve with this position is enough to kill you."

"I'll never know." Roni could not take her eyes away from the empty space in the kitchen where Darin had stood. "Gram will kill me first. Especially if she finds out about this." That thought jolted her back. She glared and pointed her finger at both men. "Not a word to her. You understand me? Not a single word. Promise me."

"You think we want to tell her any of this?" Elliot said.

"We are here with you. As far as she's concerned, we are accomplices."

Roni's cellphone rang, and before she looked, she knew the name that would be on the screen — Jane Lander. "You two search this place. See if you can find anything useful." She took a deep breath and accepted the call. "Hi, Jane."

"I want to speak with my son."

She expected that — hoped it wouldn't happen, but the day's luck clearly had been used up. "I thought you were going to drive over here to see him." Stalling seemed about the only good approach.

"Never you mind about what I'm doing. Now put my son on the phone this instant."

"I'm sorry, I can't. I'm not inside the apartment."

"You left him there alone?"

"I'm downstairs on the street getting something from my car. I'll be back up there in a minute. He's a big boy, and he's doing a lot better."

Sully and Elliot's idea of "searching the apartment" leaned more towards the idea of "tossing the apartment." They rifled through drawers, sifted paperwork, and threw cushions aside with such abandon, Roni wondered if they had ever gone through police training when they were younger.

"I'll wait," Jane said. "Put him on the phone."

Gesturing to the phone, Roni mouthed a plea for help, but Sully and Elliot shrugged. Without a good option, Roni chose a classic form of evasion. "I'm sorry, Jane, what was that? You're breaking up. I think my phone is dying. I'll try to call you soon." She ended the call.

"Nothing is here," Sully said.

Pocketing her phone, Roni went back to the kitchen — the last place she had seen Darin. She surveyed the room for any sign of what he had been thinking or where he might ... she smacked her forehead. "I'm such an idiot. I know where he's going — the zoo."

"Lots of zoos," Sully said.

"The Philadelphia Zoo."

Elliot pulled a laptop from underneath the couch. "Not quite," he said and he displayed the screen to the others. "Looks like he signed up for an Uber account. And he has Google Maps focused on the Baltimore Zoo."

"Baltimore? Why go there when the Philly Zoo is so much closer?"

"You said he was thinking clearer for a time. Perhaps he started thinking clearly again. If I needed to get to a zoo, any zoo, and I had already expressed to you that desire —"

"Then you wouldn't go where you know I'll end up searching for you."

"Precisely." Elliot checked the website again. "He has had about a forty-five minute lead on us. We should be moving now."

"Paper," Sully said, snapping his fingers at a notepad on the kitchen counter. "And a pen."

Roni swiped the pad and a pen, handed them over, and the three went to her car. As she sped down the highway toward Baltimore, she kept one eye on her rearview mirror — not watching the cars, but rather watching Sully. He sat in the backseat with his pad and pen.

Starting at the right of the page and working left, he wrote several words in Hebrew. When he finished, he removed the page from the pad and folded it. Sometimes in half, sometimes unfolding and refolding from a different start point, sometimes only crossing a small portion of the page. After a few moments, he had produced an origami crane.

He opened the car window and lifted the crane. Though

Roni knew what would come next, she still found it astonishing. Sully brought the crane's head close in and whispered to it. Seconds later, the paper bird flapped its wings and soared out the window. With barely a pause, Sully picked up the pen and started over. By the time they spotted signs announcing The Baltimore Zoo, Sully had made and released ten cranes.

After nothing but silence, Elliot cleared his throat. "Are you doing okay?"

"Me?" Roni said. "Yeah, I'm fine."

"I meant with all that you have learned and with Lillian. The last time we talked you had a big decision to make. Now, it seems you have come to regret that decision."

"I don't know. I mean I don't regret it — I'm glad I know the truth — but at the same time, I don't know. It's like Santa Claus."

Elliot had the polite grace not to laugh. "How is that?"

"When you're a kid — well, not you and not Sully, but when you're a Christian kid — parents will tell you the whole Santa Claus story. Then one day, somewhere along the line, you learn the truth, and so far as that goes, usually you're okay. The world existed in one way before and now it's become something altogether different, but it's okay. In fact, you might even be grateful to know the reality of the world. That's how I felt learning all about you guys and the books and the universes and all."

"Are you going to say that some kids regret learning about Santa Claus?"

"No. But some kids, once they do learn the truth, realize a larger, more horrible truth. They understand that for years, their parents lied to them. Sure, it was all in fun and playfulness and giving presents and all, but they lied. The two people that child expected nothing but truth from lied about something so inconsequential and kept that lie going for years. What, then, would those same people do when a serious problem arose? Does that make sense?"

"I think so."

"It's not just being lied to, either. What really screws up those kids — the ones who see the full truth — is that they are then expected to be complicit in continuing the lie. I figured out on my own that Santa was a myth and when I told Gram, she asked that I don't tell any of the other kids. She said that they might not know yet and that I shouldn't spoil it for them."

"Ah," Elliot said. "And here we are telling you to keep all of this secret. But, of course, this is not a holiday game resulting in presents. Our secret is dangerous information."

"Don't you think if Darin had known that information, it might have saved him from ever going near that book? He would have known to be careful around such things, known the consequences of opening the book, maybe he even would have turned down the job because of it."

"It's good that you question these things. It's good that you think this way. That is one reason it is always necessary to bring in young minds. But old minds know a lot, too. We have experience. The dilemma that you describe is not new. It has been argued out for centuries. Sadly, I have to tell you that nobody has come up with a satisfactory solution."

"What then? Am I supposed to roll over and accept that it sucks and that's it?"

"Not at all. In fact, you should do quite the opposite."

"Huh?"

"I told you that this has been argued for a long time. That is because there have always been people like yourself, passionate people, caring and empathetic people, who are willing to argue, to debate, to fight. Without that, those who wish to impose their will on others win."

Roni's face scrunched up. "How did we suddenly get to

fighting the establishment? Is there an establishment? I thought it was just you three."

"Did you already forget that we are called in by religious groups to investigate? There are others, too. Governments, sometimes. Private groups. I would not go so far as to suggest that there is an actual establishment, but there are people out there thinking, discussing, and debating the bigger questions of what we do — including how much to keep a secret."

"Great. How does any of that help me?"

Elliot gave a knowing grin. "Because, you see, your decision is not as Earth-shattering as you fear. Make a choice. Be part of this, whole-heartedly, or do not. It is easy. Most decisions are. They only feel difficult when you waffle between your choices."

Pointing to their exit, Roni said, "Saved by the zoo."

"The decision will not go away."

"I know." She followed the winding road into the parking area and picked a spot under the shade of a tall tree. "But right now, we have to figure out where to find Darin in this place. I've been here before. It's big. We better get started or we might be here all night."

Sully snickered. "Wait a moment, please."

"We've already lost most of the day. Let's go."

"Such impatience. Only a little longer. A short wait. I promise. Please."

Roni looked to Elliot for support but he closed his eyes with a calm demeanor as if waiting for a few days in this car was well within his ability. "Is this how you usually run an operation?"

Keeping his eyes closed, Elliot said, "There is no *usually* in this business. We have learned that the only thing we can trust is each other. If Sully tells me that we need to wait, then we wait. I trust him."

Though every muscle in her body itched to get moving, Roni eased back in her seat. "Okay. We wait."

True to his word, the wait did not take long. Only a few minutes had passed before Sully opened his hand at the window. One of his paper cranes flew in and perched on his palm. He stroked its head before whispering to it. In the next breath, the crane stopped moving — it had become nothing but paper once more.

Working with deliberate motions, Sully unfolded the paper. Roni studied the care he put into each step of his process — it was more than a magic gift to him. He treated his work with reverence and love. She guessed that when he had faced the decision to join or not, he had no problems — because Sully knew himself, understood his own heart. Then again, he projected that surety now. Back when he was her age or younger, he may have been more conflicted. After all, he had admitted that it took him a while to accept the shift in reality, so perhaps he had trouble with the bigger questions, too.

Did that mean that eventually she would discover the self-assured confidence Sully and Elliot now displayed? And did they only acquire that through this kind of work?

"Here we are," Sully said.

On the paper, flattened out on his lap, Roni saw the Hebrew words. However, these were not the same as the ones that Sully had written. Though she could not read Hebrew, she could see easily enough that the handwriting and the number of words had changed.

Elliot shifted in his seat so that he could look directly at Sully. "Okay, friend. You have had your moment. Now tell us what the birdie said."

Sully winked. "I thought you had the patience and the trust for me."

"I do. I also know that when the spotlight is on you,

there are times when you like to linger in its shine. However, as our dear Roni has made clear, we should consider our limited time. Therefore, I ask you again with the greatest of respect, what did the birdie say?"

"Very well. Mr. Lander is at the wolf exhibit. He went right there from the start and sits there still. That is where we go."

Roni rested her chin on the back of her seat as she looked at the paper. "That's weird."

"All of this is weird," Elliot said. "If you stick with it, you get used to weird."

"I mean it's weird that he picked the wolf exhibit to go catatonic again. When he was like that in the kitchen, he focused on the animal picture on the wall, but it was of lions. I sort of expected him to go to the lion exhibit."

Elliot shook his head as he pondered Roni's words.

Sully shrugged. "I only tell you what the crane told me. Wolf, lion — does it really matter? Each world we touch is unique in some way. Some more than others. Who's to say what we should expect?"

"I guess," Roni said. "But how do you prepare for any of this, then? How do we know what to do with Darin?"

"We don't," Elliot said. "We know how the books work. And the cavern."

"And our gifts," Sully added.

"Yes, our gifts, too. The things that exist in our universe are the things that we do understand. But when we must deal with another universe — by that, I mean more than locking it away into a book. Rather I mean something like we are dealing with now, with Darin — well, when we must handle these kinds of situations, we rely on the things we do know and improvise the rest."

Roni drummed her hands on her seat as she opened the door. "Anybody ever tell you that you use a lot of words to say the simplest things?"

"Our friend in the backseat often tells me so."

Sully rubbed the back of his hand against the loose skin under his neck. "Ignore him. We have work to do. Eyes open. This could be dangerous."

The playfulness in their banter had lulled Roni into forgetting the seriousness of the situation. Only for a second or two, but it left her with a sense of being unprepared. As they exited the car and headed toward the main gate, she tried to convince herself that entering with two seasoned veterans ready to face anything would be enough — no matter how old they were. Watching Sully shuffling along the way and seeing how Elliot leaned heavier on his cane than before did not inspire her with confidence.

CHAPTER 15

When they bought tickets to enter the zoo, the cashier raised an eyebrow. "The zoo is going to close in about an hour."

"That's okay," Roni said. "We won't be long. Just looking to get some exercise in these old bones."

"Who you calling old?" Sully said.

The cashier chuckled and handed over the tickets. As they walked in, droves of haggard parents and sugar-high kids meandered out through the exit turnstiles. They wore baseball caps with flamingos attached to the visor, sported new t-shirts displaying the zoo logo, and carried bags full of toys and games — all zoo themed, of course.

The welcome area had a large fountain as the centerpiece of an open air section. Roni walked over to a large map of the zoo and pointed off to the right. The two men followed her.

Elliot gazed ahead as they walked by gibbons on one side and eagles on the other. He chuckled — a soft rumble deep in his throat — and said, "I do not know if you will recall this, but when you were a girl, maybe six or seven, your grandmother and I brought you here for a day."

Shaking her head, Roni said, "I don't remember a lot from those years."

"I know. It is hard to hold onto memories when you have suffered the loss of a parent. I wish you could remember that day, though. It is a happy memory. You were like a bee, buzzing along, hopping from one flower to the next — except these flowers were the exhibits. You loved it. And down at the bottom of the hill — I do not know if it is still there — they had a mini-train to take the children around part of the zoo. When your grandmother mentioned this, you were enthralled. *Choo-choo.* You said it over and over in every possible variation of pitches. *Choo-choo.* We laughed about that for a long time."

They moved at a steady albeit slow pace. Roni did not mind. The extra time gave the stragglers a chance to exit the zoo. That meant less people around when they confronted Darin. Should he not leave with them willingly, should he lash out or behave aggressively, there would be less people to get in the way.

After about seven minutes of walking, they reached the wolf enclosure. Darin sat on a wooden bench facing the wolves. Tall trees shaded the brick path and a trashcan decorated with wood slats stood a few feet away. A sign above the trashcan read: *Don't be an animal. Throw away your trash.*

If not for Darin's harrowing experience and his unstable state of mind, Roni would have thought she looked upon a man's serene moment of quiet contemplation. Perhaps she had. Though she felt dread and danger around her, that only existed because the Old Gang told her this would be dangerous. Not exactly true, though. She still shivered when she thought of all she saw within that book. So, even if Darin meant no harm, she knew the Old Gang was right to be cautious. She just didn't want it to be that way.

Nudging her shoulder, Elliot said, "Go talk with him."

"Are you serious? Isn't that like walking into the lion's den?"

"Sully and I need to clear the area before we can make a move." He indicated a couple walking hand-in-hand and an old woman with her dog. "As well, you clearly have some connection with him."

"Maybe. But —"

"Did he harm you when you took him to his mother's place?"

"No."

"Did he harm you when you found him walking on the road?"

"No."

"Did he harm you at his apartment? Or while you slept?"

"No. I get it. I'll go talk to him. What am I trying to do? Just distract him?"

"Distraction is a good start. Keep him calm. From what you have described, he goes in and out of lucidity. Right now, I would guess that he is not aware of much. Perhaps hearing your voice will bring him back to consciousness. If so, then try to talk him into leaving with us. That would be the ideal. Otherwise, stick with distraction, and we will handle it from there."

Elliot snapped his fingers at Sully and the two men walked ahead. Elliot approached the woman with the dog while Sully smiled at the couple. Roni tried to stay focused on Darin.

When she stepped in front of him, she first noticed that he did not appear to be in contemplative meditation. Instead, he looked like a couch potato too lazy to change the channel from a nature show to something more lively. She wiggled her fingers in an attempt at a cute *hello* wave but saw no reaction.

A strange, sharp flicker of light — amber and orange — crossed his skin. She turned her head toward the sky but the sun had begun to set. It could not have caused that bright flicker. She waited to see if it happened again, but nothing changed.

As if he had woken from an afternoon nap, Darin took in his surroundings as he stretched his arms. "Hi, there. Have a seat."

Roni settled on the bench but kept her feet ready to spring away. "How are you feeling?"

"Better and better. It's taken me longer than I expected to get comfortable with this reality."

"Tell me about it. You spend your whole life thinking up is up and down is down, and by doing nothing more than opening a book, it's all different. I can't begin to imagine what you must think since you actually went in there."

"Book? I mean the reality around us, not some story."

Did he not remember? "Of course. This is quite different from inside the ... that is, from where you were."

"Beautiful creatures, aren't they?" He watched the wolves as they watched him. "Working in concert together, following a hierarchy that keeps them safe and functional. That's a reality which makes sense."

"It's certainly less complicated than what we deal with. I don't even know where to start with you. I want to assure you that we can help you, but I don't even know if we can help me. I don't mean that in a self-centered way. I only meant — oh, forget it. I'm screwing this all up."

"You're fine. I should apologize to you. I'm sure my earlier behavior was disturbing."

"I guess." She found his current behavior more disturbing but kept quiet.

"It was difficult, at first, to function in a new reality.

Difficult to get my new way of thinking to respond to my old understanding of the way the world worked."

"I've been going through it, too. It's like there's this battle going on inside my head. I look around and it all seems like it was but then there's this other layer of knowing what else is out there, things most people will never see, but I've seen them and I can't forget them and I think I'm babbling." She giggled. "I'm sorry."

"You know, Darin really liked you."

"What?"

"On your date the other night. Even though he used you to gain access to the basement, he really liked you. I thought you might like to know that."

Roni's mouth went dry. She inched further to the edge of the bench, ready to bolt. "Darin told you that?"

"Oh, yes."

"Does that mean you're not Darin?"

The amber-orange light flickered again, only this time Roni saw it clearly — coming from under Darin's skin. He grinned. "I am so much more."

In the distance, Roni spotted Elliot taking up a position that both flanked Darin and cut off one of the exit paths from this section of the zoo. She suspected Sully did the same behind her.

Attempting to maintain her composure, she said, "You know, when people start talking about themselves in the third person, often it means they're a bit crazy. But I don't think that's the case with you."

"I appreciate that."

"In fact, I think you're being absolutely sincere. I mean you honestly are not Darin anymore. So, I'm guessing you came from that other world. Right? You saw Darin in there, and you did something to him, jumped inside of him somehow, and then came out here like a stowaway."

"Not quite." His skin flickered again — more intensely this time. "I did not jump inside the man. I copied him. As much as I could in the time given. Once I arrived here, it took me more time to figure out how his mind functioned — language skills, in particular, are difficult. But here I am."

Roni frowned. "You're a copy of Darin?"

"I am."

"Then what happened to Darin?"

"I left him. Locked away in my world, just as I am locked away here. Though I certainly ended up with the better situation."

Swallowing against her dry throat, she asked, "What now? You planning to live your life as one of us?"

"Don't be disgusting." Again the light beneath his skin flickered. Shadows of his bone structure appeared in the stronger light. "I can do so much better."

Roni called upon all her will power to remain seated. She feared any sudden action — like running for her life — might startle this creature, perhaps trigger a predator/prey instinct. "Maybe you should relax a little. You don't look too well."

Darin jerked to his feet. "I feel better than I have since I was born." He faced Roni — his eyes manic, his gestures broad, his skin flickering like an orange strobe light. "I spent my whole life in that ooze. Fighting to eat. Fighting to breathe. Fighting to mate. That world is nothing like this. This is superior in every way."

The wolves rushed to the edge of their cage. Some growled. Others barked. Their attention solely on Darin. He watched them again, his fascination unending.

Something tugged on Roni's arm. She looked over to see Sully. Even as she wondered how he had managed to sneak up so close without being detected, she found her legs unwilling to move.

Darin snapped his focus onto Sully. With a vicious bark of his own, Darin lashed out. He moved fast, his fingers locking on Sully's thin wrist and twisting hard. Sully groaned as he bent further over in pain.

"Run," he managed, but Roni could only watch.

Darin squeezed tighter, his eyes blazing with anger and curiosity as if he wondered how long it would take to break Sully's wrist. He never got to find out.

A blinding sun burst before him — Elliot stood in the way, his cane a glowing mass of light. He pressed forward, and Darin had no choice but to back off. Freed from Darin's vice grip, Sully scurried off toward the exit, nursing his wounded hand.

"Come on, Roni," Elliot yelled as he pushed his cane at Darin.

"I-I can't move."

To Darin, Elliot said, "Release her!"

But no magic constrained Roni. Fear kept her frozen. Fear and a bizarre sensation — kinship? No. That seemed too strong. But something inside her refused to let her move.

Elliot tried to yank her to her feet, but he couldn't get her to budge. The wolves howled from their cage. Elliot glanced over, and Roni knew the animals had created a diversion. Darin lunged forward, gnarling his teeth as he bowled into Elliot. The two rolled on the ground until Darin popped up, straddling the old man. Two strong punches, and Elliot went limp.

Darin glared at Sully until it became clear that the fight had ended. He then walked toward the wolf cage. "Where I'm from, these men would be dead, but I want to show you that I can adapt."

Elliot rolled on his side. The days of Sully and Elliot

punching their way through problems had ended long ago, but they did not want to admit it. Roni wondered if she acted similar — that Darin presented a new reality and she did not want to admit it.

"Adaptation is the most important skill in my world." Darin unbuttoned his shirt revealing a smooth chest with sparse definition. "I want you to see. I can adapt to your world, I will adapt, better than any living thing you have here."

"What are you saying?" Roni asked.

"Watch and see."

With one hand, he squeezed his fingers together and compressed them against his stomach. As if his skin has been made of gelatin, his hand slipped through. Roni's eyes dried from not blinking, but she could not force a change. She had to watch.

He dug around within his body for a moment, grunted as he gripped something, and pulled his hand free. The skin around his stomach sealed, leaving behind no scar. In his palm, he held a bright amber-orange goo. It glowed and snapped out light at odd times. It undulated.

Roni's brain shrieked at her, pleaded with her, demanded that she move. She had to get up, turn around, and run. Sprint. Get the hell out of there.

She stayed motionless.

"Is that you?" she asked.

It flickered faster. Roni looked to Darin, but his face had gone slack, his eyes empty. But his body moved.

He stepped toward the wolves. They stood on their hind legs, whining and scratching like domesticated dogs begging to be let outside.

Roni's body numbed as her brain attempted to place this image into her concept of reality — new or old. But even in her new reality, human beings could not do what she had witnessed.

She reminded herself that this thing before her looked like Darin but could not be called human. The real Darin still suffered within the universe in the book. This impostor could not be counted upon to follow the behavior and physical attributes of a human being. The glowing puddle in his hand proved as much. If she doubted any of her thoughts, he made it undeniable in the next seconds.

Darin leaned over the railing, stretching his arm as close to the wolf cage as possible. One wolf, a gray and black hulking animal — the Alpha — shoved its snout between the bars. Whimpering, it pushed harder in an attempt to reach Darin. Like a lightning bolt, arcing and twisting, the puddle of muck in Darin's hand shot out and latched upon the wolf's nose.

Without a sound, the rest of the pack sat on their haunches like obedient, well-trained police canines. The gray and black Alpha tried to retreat, but the glowing goo kept the animal locked in place. The wolf snarled as it foamed at the mouth. Its breathing shortened as if the animal struggled underwater until finally succumbing to the inevitable. The muck stretching between Darin and the wolf detached and languidly returned to its puddle form in Darin's hand.

With casual grace, Darin slipped the undulating goo back into his abdomen. Arching back, he dangled his hands at his side. Roni swore the man's face had changed. His mouth thrust forward as he inhaled deeply and let loose a long, wailing howl. The pack of wolves lifted their heads and sang notes of their own as his personal chorus.

When he straightened and looked upon Roni, her fears had been confirmed. His face had transformed. He had taken on many wolf-like qualities — his mouth and nose pushed forward, whiskers poked out from the sides, hair grew along his jawline, his teeth had lengthened and sharpened.

He put out his hand. "I have no intention of being alone here. You were the first, the only one of this world to show me kindness. I shall reciprocate. Come with me, and I will make you better than you are. Better than anybody from this world."

Recoiling, Roni found the strength to say, "I like being human just fine."

Darin growled, and the pack barked and growled in concert. They jumped over each other. They scratched and gnawed at the bars in an endless attempt to break through.

"You will come with me, or you will suffer."

"Not a good line to win me over."

He furrowed his brow in thought. "Ah, *suffer* is the wrong word. I meant that if you do not come with me, you will be my victim."

"Not really any better."

"Then you will die."

The threat of death finally broke the mixture of fear and amazement that had kept Roni rooted to the bench. She leaped to her feet and sprinted for the exit behind her. The snorting snarls chased after her along with Darin. Ahead, Sully and Elliot stood like two action heroes past their prime. Not the most comforting image, but better than nothing.

To her surprise, Sully stepped forward. He gestured toward Darin as Elliot hunched like a linebacker ready to catch Roni. Peeking around Elliot's arm, Roni watched as all of Sully's paper cranes soared in. They circled Darin's head, dive-bombed his body, and pecked at his skin. Pricks of blood dotted his arms and face.

"Go! Go!" Sully said.

The three hurried back up the path, leaving Darin

swatting at the nerveless attackers.

"No way will that stop him for long," Roni said.

"True," Elliot said. "But he will not follow us further." Proving his point, Elliot slowed his pace.

"He wants to kill me."

"We have seen this before. There is a madness that strikes some when they travel between worlds. He sees our home, and it is more beautiful, more bountiful, more innocent than whatever existence he endured before. In his madness, he desires all of it."

"Including me."

"Perhaps. But desiring an entire world outweighs chasing down one woman."

Sully wiped his glasses with the bottom of his shirt. "Usually."

Elliot nodded. "Usually. The birds stopped him long enough to get some distance, and since he has not attacked us yet, I suspect my interpretation of his mental state and attitudes is correct."

Fluttering her shirt to cool down, Roni said, "Can we get the heck out of here?"

"Certainly. We must soon return to the bookshop and report to your grandmother."

Roni stopped. "We don't need to tell her any of this."

"I am afraid we can no longer keep this secret. We must have her help."

Roni slumped as they trudged uphill toward the parking lot. "Great."

CHAPTER 16

The big table in the middle of the bookstore's main floor had always been a joyful place for Roni. As a girl, she would bring her stack of books to the table and let the day drift by between their pages. As a teen, she would sneak a boy underneath the table for a stolen kiss, and in later years, for more. But as an adult, sitting on one side along Sully and Elliot, the table made her feel small and foolish. Gram's beady-eyed rage probably had something to do with that, too.

"Of all the stupid, idiotic, addled-brained things to do!" Gram paced the length of the table as she blasted her sternest looks at each of the men. "I can comprehend on some ridiculously childish level why Roni would think that going off to face this creature without any sort of plan or forethought might be a good idea, but you two? You should have known better. Haven't you had enough bad experiences to know that your little foray into stupidity would end badly?"

Sully's top lip lifted. "You would rather we left your granddaughter to face all of that alone?"

"Don't you dare try to pretend that this was all in her

best interest. If that were true, you would have come to me, told me what was going on, and we could have dealt with it together — as a team. You remember that concept? We're supposed to act like a team instead of going behind my back."

"Teammates don't give ultimatums."

Gram's face reddened even as her eyes blazed. "You're going to lecture me now on the choices I give my granddaughter?"

Elliot splayed his fingers wide on the tabletop. In a thoughtful delivery, he said, "I believe you know that Sully did not mean that. Rather, he is trying to point out to you, in his own way, that you should be less upset that we did this *behind your back* and more concerned with what circumstances existed in which Roni felt it necessary to enlist our aid without you."

"Oh? Is that right? I see. After all these years raising her into a bright and capable woman, I'm suddenly no longer a good judge of her best interests. She's facing a shift in how she will perceive the world from this point to the end of her life, a shift I myself made decades ago, but I don't have the skill to guide her through it. Is that what you're trying to say?"

Though he continued to speak calmly, the mounted tension could not be missed. If not in his voice, then certainly in his fingers. They clawed into the table as he spoke. "I always have said the words I mean to say. Your inability to understand them or willfully misinterpret them is something I have no control over."

"Enough," Roni said. She tried to stand but Gram's cold glare kept her seated. "You all can argue about me when I'm not around."

"Young lady," Gram said, thumping the table with a meaty fist, "I don't think you are in a position to —"

"You're wrong. I'm in the perfect position because I am the one at risk here. Darin isn't interested in coming after you or Sully or Elliot. He wants me — either to love or kill, he may not even know, but he wants me."

"Then why did he let you go?"

"Maybe he believes in the old *set it free and see if it comes back* kind of love."

"Perhaps," Elliot said, "we should focus on steps forward."

"I would love to do that," Gram said, "but unfortunately, my granddaughter and my two imbecilic friends decided to challenge a creature from another universe before knowing the first thing about it and what it can do."

"I only meant that —"

"I know, I know. I'm not done yelling yet. Can I have that? Is that okay with you? Or if I don't shut up and follow your lead on this, do it exactly how you think it should be done, are you going to go off and take Roni and Sully behind my back again?"

Breathing hard, Gram glowered at them. Nobody said a word.

She looked off to the side, her face going through several awkward motions as if she had a conversation with herself. "Well, I guess I'm done." She sat at the table. "Now, if I can trust that you've all learned your lesson here and that you'll be more open, more forthcoming, in the future, let's get moving forward on this. Do we know where Darin is right now?"

"No," Roni said. "I would hazard a guess that he's either back at his apartment or at his mother's house. Those were the places he went before."

"He also went to the zoo. And those places were part of Darin, not this creature. He only went there to bide time while he adjusted to our world."

Sully pushed his chair back as he stood. "I'll get to work on it."

Gram wagged her hand at him. "We can't afford to waste your time on that. You need to get in your workshop and build us something to handle this. Or did you boys not get beat enough to know that you're not young anymore? The days of you knocking out a threat in one punch left us long ago."

With a bashful grimace, Sully said, "You will mock us with that for years, won't you?"

"If I'm lucky." As Sully left for the elevator, Gram turned her attention to Elliot. "I want you to track down Darin."

Elliot's mouth dropped as if he had been slapped. "Shouldn't that be Roni's job?"

"Roni has shown us that she is not ready to handle jobs on her own. Look at how she botched up this one." She raised both hands to stop anybody from talking. "She's made it clear that her only interest in helping us goes to the end of this current job, so let's not get dependent on her aid. Of course, if you don't agree with me, we have procedures for challenging the leader of the group — procedures you should have followed instead of running off to the zoo. Do you want to do that now, or can I trust that you'll follow my orders?"

Elliot grabbed his cane. "I will find this creature. When you are ready to make a move, I will have his location for you."

After Elliot left, Gram laced her fingers on the table and looked at Roni. For her part, though she felt bad for how things went down, she pulled her shoulders back and met Gram's eyes straight on. For three solid minutes, no words passed between them.

At length, Gram got to her feet and stepped toward the elevators. "Come with me."

Roni obeyed. They climbed into the elevator and Gram pressed the wall beneath the floor selector buttons. A hidden panel slid open with several more buttons on it. She pressed one button and the elevator descended. They came to the basement level but kept going until the digital display above the door read B2.

"A second basement?" Roni said.

Flashing a mischievous smile, Gram gestured to the opening elevator doors. Roni stepped into a cinderblock hallway with lamps hung periodically from the ceiling. The air reminded her of the caverns — uniformly cool with a taste both fresh and old.

Gram led the way down the hall until they reached a metal door. "This is the last time I'm going to show you any of what we have and do. You understand? There won't be another chance after this." Before Roni could protest or explain, Gram stopped her with that powerful hand in the air. "I know. You keep forgetting that I raised you. This wouldn't be the first time you've made a decision without getting all the information."

"You didn't really offer much."

She rested her hand on the door handle. "That was an unfortunate decision on my part. I know you've only seen the three of us — we are all there is now, but not all that ever was. Others came before us, and others before them. No organized group lasts as long as this one has without some bit of ceremony or tradition growing up along the way. When it came to initiating you into our fold, I had a choice to make. I could go with tradition or go with my gut. Now, my gut told me that you are impulsive and would have to make a choice and live with it for a little before you would know whether or not it was the right choice. That's how you've always been. But the tradition was to withhold most of the information and make you choose based on whatever you had experienced. I ignored my gut feeling because my brain hoped you would be different."

"Gee, thanks."

"I don't mean it like that and you know it. I only mean that I hoped there was some magic, I guess, magic in the tradition. Somehow, talking with Elliot in the morning and facing the decision to stay with us or forever give up all of this, I thought maybe it would light a fire within you that had been dormant. Like it was for me."

Roni's stomach knotted. "And I messed up for you."

"I miscalculated a little, that's all. I should have listened to my gut and known that you are who you are. I could have made this easier. But better late than never, right? You made your decision to leave us after this Darin business is over, and you've had to live with that decision for a bit of time. You may even think you know what your final decision will be."

"Gram, I'm sorry, but after all that happened, what makes you think I'll change my mind?"

"I want you to see one more of our secrets." Pushing the handle, Gram opened the door. "If you're going to turn your back on your legacy, you should know exactly what you are turning away."

They stepped into a beautiful library room decorated as if it belonged to an aristocrat in the nineteenth century. High-ceiling, Turkish rugs, handcrafted tables and chairs, wood walls with original oil paintings hanging in gold frames — each one a portrait, Gram explained, of former members in the Parallel Society.

"That's our official name," she said.

Off to the left, Roni saw a wine rack filled with dusty bottles. Though there were two computers humming away on the tables, an old card catalog had been placed off to the right. And, of course, there were books. Hundreds of them. They overflowed the shelves, stacked up on the floor, lined the tops of every surface. Some were leatherbound, some with metal covers, and a few had no cover at all but were scrolls tied with strips of cloth.

Gram eased into one of the chairs. "Everything that's vital to us is in here. Books on every subject we've ever found important. Many of the books are the only copies in existence. But more importantly, we have all the diaries and journals of our former members. That's a key part of our job. We document everything. Hundreds of years of information can be found in this library."

Roni found herself both amazed and appalled. "How do you find anything in here?"

"It was better organized long ago. We haven't had a good librarian for ages."

"I see. You thought I would do this work."

"I remember how you were with your school books. You'd have them lined on your shelf, sometimes based on size, sometimes alphabetically, sometimes I don't know what. But you were always keeping good order to things."

Roni shook her head and laughed. "Have you seen my apartment? It's a sty." Except for her bookshelf, but Roni didn't want to give Gram any extra ammunition.

"There's often a difference between the way one lives and the way one works. I've seen you work in the bookstore. I know that you would love taking care of this place."

She had to admit Gram's words held some truth. "I don't know."

"Don't decide yet. We're doing things for you the right way this time. Experience it. Let it sit. Give it time. Besides, I didn't bring you down here just to show off the library.

We've still got the Darin business to deal with. This library is chock full of information. If there's anything that can help us handle Darin, we'll find it in here."

Leaning forward, Gram cleared some yellowed papers off of another chair. Part of Roni resisted the idea of taking that seat. She had a sudden fear that if she sat down, she might never leave this room again. She might look up and discover she had aged forty years, her life had become nothing but dealing with these books and papers, that all the excitement of the last few days would be nothing but a memory.

But Gram had one thing right — Roni made better decisions when she dove in and experienced a thing. She sat, clapped her hands against her knees, and grinned. "Let's get to work."

CHAPTER 17

When Roni got involved with a book, the rest of the world slipped away. She absorbed the words, internalized them, and made them real — in some cases, more real than the outside world. Even with non-fiction, she could delve in between the letters and words and punctuation to find the world beneath the words.

As the hours drifted by, Roni and Gram combed over book after book, and throughout it all, Roni relished each treasured word like a connoisseur of fine wines. Most of these books had never been read by anyone other than those few souls who were brought to this special room. In some cases, the books had never been read at all. The robust aroma of the old paper, the crinkling of it as she turned the pages, the weight of each volume in her lap — it combined to make an experience she knew she would never have again. Even as she sought vital information, part of her brain tried to savor the moment itself, tried to record it within its firing neurons. This was something to remember until her final breath.

After another hour, Gram stretched her legs. She mumbled about a coffee machine, and a few minutes later uncovered the relic sitting behind a rolling cart full of books. A few minutes of fiddling and a quick trip upstairs for ground coffee beans, and Gram served up two hot mugs of caffeine.

Once Gram got back to reading, Roni took a lap around the library to get the blood flowing through to her legs. In the back corner, she found two tall shelving units that had been set up in an L-shape, closing off the area. They looked odd, and it took Roni a moment to figure out why — something was behind them.

The tall ceiling meant that none of the shelving units went all the way to the top. Roni could see clearly that the room continued beyond these shelves. Peeking over a few books, she could make a dark shape, perhaps a table, and little else.

Picking the smaller of the two shelves, she removed every book in it — making sure to check the titles in case anything might be useful for the Darin situation. She stacked them in order so they could be refiled with ease. Once emptied, she reached in, grabbed hold of the shelf, and lifted one side of the unit.

Though heavy enough to elicit a hearty grunt, the shelving unit pivoted inward close to a foot. Holding her stomach in, Roni slipped through the opening and discovered a table with rolls of paper. She spread them open, one after the other. Maps. Each one depicted part of the caverns. In many instances, numerical codes designated the various books chained to the walls. In some cases, entire areas had a marking with names like *Painted Worlds, Unbreathable,* and *Carlson's Journey.*

"Ah, the maps," Gram said, leaning her back against the shelving unit while she sipped her coffee. "There are more somewhere around here."

"More? How big is this cavern?"

"Don't know for sure. I have no doubt you could fit entire cities in here."

Roni's fingers traced one path after the other. Near the bottom of each map, she saw the cartographer's name along with the words *The Parallel Society*. "Why do you call yourselves that when these aren't parallel universes? Are they?"

"Not in the sense of another Roni, another Sully and Elliot, another me running around. And you won't find another Earth where Hitler won the war or the Industrial Revolution never happened or anything like that. As far as I can tell from what I've read in here, these worlds are not alternates to our own, but rather co-existing universes, each unique unto itself."

"Then why *The Parallel Society?* That seems wrong."

"I didn't name it. Perhaps back in the 1400s, that was the best way they could understand what was going on. Who knows? But for whatever reason, that was the name the original founders of the Society chose, and it's stayed with us."

"The 1400s? This thing goes back that far?"

"Maybe further. I suppose the answer is somewhere in this library, but we haven't had a dedicated librarian down here for a long time. So, things get hard to know."

"I can see that."

Roni opened another map, and near the center, she noticed a roughly circular area. Usually that sort of section marked a manmade pool that gathered water from natural, underground streams — she had seen quite a few on the other maps — but this time the words *Lost Memories* had been written in, along with several numerical notations near the symbol for books.

"What does this mean?" she asked.

Gram craned her neck to see without moving. "Oh,

nothing. There are a ton of fanciful names the mapmakers used. Most are mere flourishes more evocative than meaningful."

"There's no way you can read what I'm pointing out from over there."

Gram's mouth thinned. "I can see the type of thing you're pointing at, even if I can't read the specific words. Grab any map and you'll see many similar labels."

"But this one says *Lost Memories*. What kind of worlds can that mean? Or is something else there?"

"Right now, it doesn't matter. We need to stay focused."

Roni read those words again. "I have lost memories. Lost time — that's what you've always called them."

"Look at those maps long enough and you'll see infinite answers to infinite questions. It's like tarot cards or astrology. You can interpret those writings to mean whatever you want them to mean — none of which will help Darin."

"Maybe."

"Even if you found some proof that the labels meant something real, you'd still have to go find the place. Map or no map, these caverns are not easy to navigate. More than one Society member went in there looking for some answer and never returned."

Roni brushed the words *Lost Memories* before rolling the paper back up. Gram was right. The maps were disorganized, and Roni had no idea how they connected. She had no way to know what route to take in order to find that area nor what to do should she actually locate this specific pool.

Together, they returned to their books. Roni delved into the daily journal of Nigel Cuthbert, a Londoner who came to America in 1807 at the request of his Aunt Millicent. Three years later, he learned of and joined the Society.

Roni had picked out this journal because earlier in the day, she had read a short chapbook entitled, *A Discussion Regarding Doppelgangers and Their Multitudinous Primal Forms*. The chapbook read more like wishful thinking or creative interpretation, but considering the strange, new reality Roni found herself in, she could not discount anything outright. Still, Mr. Cuthbert's writing on the subject had numerous open-ended questions and winding paths that lead to no conclusion. Roni hoped that she would come across mention of glowing puddles of ooze, but when it came to primal forms, Mr. Cuthbert had to admit he never encountered such a thing. Worse, in his final paragraph, he admitted that he never encountered a doppelganger and that the entire book contained his best estimation of the possibilities.

That had been a waste of time earlier, but she needed something humorous to clear her head. She hoped Mr. Cuthbert's daily journal would provide the levity she sought. It did.

He wrote often of a young widow who lived several blocks over. His infatuation with her grew stronger each day, and he invented reasons to visit that area as much as possible. While amusing enough to read about, Roni could not help but chuckle at his failed attempts to woo the young lady.

He brought her flowers which caused a sharp allergic reaction. He bought her a chicken and as he delivered his gift, a rabid dog chased him down, taking the food for itself. He even attempted to write her a poem but stymied himself with the word *orange*, and refused to change it no matter how long he would have to search for the perfect rhyme.

But then Roni read a sentence that caused her to bolt upright. Gram raised an eyebrow as Roni went over the passage again.

"Well?" Gram finally said when it appeared Roni would get lost in thought.

Roni's knitted brow loosened. "I think I have an idea. This fellow here is trying to win the heart of a woman, writes a poem, and gets hung up on the word *orange*. I know, but here's the thing — he writes in his journal that the word must be in the poem because, *'it was over that rare fruit in which I first saw her. It is no more or less than a talisman to call her heart to mine.'* A talisman. That's our answer."

"How so?"

"You had me get a deeply personal item of Darin's — the ticket stub — and we used it to lure him back to the Golem so he could come back to our world."

"Except that isn't him."

"Really? What proof do we have? None. The only thing suggesting that Darin is not Darin is, well, Darin."

Gram sipped her coffee and crossed her legs. "I'm fairly certain that the Darin you went on a date with did not have the ability to turn partly into a wolf."

"I'm not saying Darin is one hundred percent the human being that went into that book. I'm saying that he did come out and that this creature inside him is a parasite. Who else but Darin would be lured by that ticket stub?"

"Okay. Let's say you're right. Where does that get us?"

"To the next logical question — if Darin is really here, then why did he lie about it? I mean, why did his parasite force him to lie? I think that parasite is controlling him. It couldn't at first, it needed time to take over, but once it did, then Darin was more of a traveler in the backseat of his own body."

"I hear a lot of supposition and see nothing in the way of evidence."

"Isn't that why I'm here, though? To read these books,

put ideas together, and come up with possible answers. I mean, you know we're not going to find a book that says the answer is X. If that answer existed, we could have stopped all of this a long time ago."

Gram gestured to the disorganized heaps of books. "Are you not seeing the mess here?"

"I do. But Darin — the real Darin — snuck into the caverns and picked out a specific book. It had to be a specific book because otherwise he could have grabbed much closer and easier to reach books. So, whoever hired him knew about that book. All of that means the answer is not hidden away down here where nobody can get to it or everybody forgot about it — clearly somebody knows about this particular book and what can be found in it."

Gram set her coffee down and leaned forward. "Are you suggesting that somebody wanted Darin to have this parasite in him?"

"To bring it back here."

"It's a chilling thought. And you might be right. All the more reason we have to stop Darin before he has a chance to do whatever he intends. Him or whoever hired him — which is a bigger question for another time."

Roni bounced on the edge of her seat as she pointed in the journal. "If I'm right about Darin, then I'm pretty sure the answer is in the talisman. It was his personal connection to that ticket stub which gave him the strength or the will power to find his way back."

"And you think he can do it again. Only this time instead of clawing his way to a Golem and out of that book, he'd be clawing his way back into commanding his own body."

"I think so."

Gram leaned closer to read the passage from Cuthbert's journal. "Perhaps. But we have a problem. The ticket stub doesn't exist anymore. It was destroyed with the Golem."

"Lucky for us, he didn't go to that game alone. There's a second stub. But you'll have to come with me to get it. No way will Darin's mother hand over that other stub to me."

Gram's eyes widened. She stood and stepped behind Roni. Patting her granddaughter on the shoulder, she said, "I think we can work that out."

CHAPTER 18

Halfway to Lancaster, Roni's nerves fired off. Her fingers tap-tap-tapped against the steering wheel while her heart tap-tap-tapped against her chest. "Are you sure you're okay with this?" she asked Gram.

"Dear, I hate to spoil your image of me, but this isn't my first time doing this kind of thing. Not even my tenth. If you're uncomfortable, that's perfectly fine. We can switch roles. I've done both parts, so it doesn't matter to me."

Roni shook her head. "Better not. If Darin's mother sees me, she'll probably call the police."

"That wouldn't do. Best to keep the plan as is."

Though it would be a solid thirty minutes before they turned into the housing development, to Roni it felt like three. The pale moon cast a dim light across the dark, and the night felt thick. Despite the streetlights and a few houses with signs of life, the shadows encroached upon every surface like hands reaching out. Roni tried to clear her mind of such ominous thoughts, but she could not stop — every shadow bore monsters to her eyes.

"Park here," Gram said. "We don't want to get so close that she recognizes your car."

Roni pulled up behind an oversized SUV. Gram unbuckled, gave Roni a reassuring squeeze on the arm, and got out. Before closing the door, she leaned in. "Give me a few minutes but please don't take too long. I hate small talk."

As she left, Roni wanted to laugh. Gram could talk for hours about anything — the more banal, the better. Either she had a false self-image or she did not understand the meaning of the phrase *small talk*.

Watching Gram waddle along the sidewalk toward Jane Lander's house, her big bag like an extra appendage at her side, Roni had an image flash in her mind. She saw how Gram must have been in her younger years — walking into danger with that same hefty confidence. That image connected to a slim memory from many years back. Gramps had yet to be ravaged by cancer, and Roni sat on his knee at a park in the summer. She asked him how had he fallen in love with Gram.

"Oh, that's quite a story," he said, his rough whiskers white against his brown skin. "A long story, too. Maybe someday, when you're much older, I can tell you all about it. Now don't get all huffy with me. I can see that stubbornness in your eye like you're planning on causing me trouble tonight — won't eat your vegetables or some kind of fuss. Calm down. I'm going to tell you what I can." He scooted her closer so that he could whisper his answer. He had warm breath. Warm breath and rough whiskers. "One of the first things I ever noticed about your Gram was the way she walked. She's a big woman, but she never thuds around. She's got style and grace and a whole mess of confidence. She knows she's worth something, always has. Back when we were young, she wasn't taking sass from nobody. Would hardly accept a date because she was waiting."

"For you?"

"I hoped so. Don't think she had me in mind, though. Naw, she was waiting for the right guy, whoever he was, the first one who would see her for the beauty she was — still is. I happen to be the lucky one — met her at the right time."

Roni remembered that moment so clearly because it changed the way she saw Gram. But it also was the only memory of Gramps that stayed with her. The rest had been lost along with so much else.

Gram turned up onto the walkway leading to the house. Almost time. Roni crossed her fingers and tried to control her breathing. She would need some of Gram's confidence tonight — any bit would do.

She checked her phone — 10:07 pm. She would have to wait at least five minutes before moving. Hopefully that would be long enough for Gram to do her part but not so long that Gram would be pissed off at having to endure small talk for any significant length. She checked her phone again — still 10:07 pm.

Five minutes — if she could get her mind thinking on something, it would go quick. But her mind blanked. She stared at the street, clenched and unclenched her fingers, and waited. Five minutes. It snailed along, giving Roni's stomach plenty of opportunity to gurgle and groan. A pain stitched up her side only to ease after she burped. She checked her phone — still that stupid 10:07 pm.

"Come on," she said. As if in snarky reply, the time moved to 10:08 pm.

Checking the side and rearview mirrors, Roni observed the street for signs of anybody coming. No need, though. The street was empty. The sidewalks were empty. From one house a few mailboxes back, a blue light flashed out from the downstairs window with no other lights on.

Probably someone fell asleep while watching television. She wondered what that life must be like — so free of worry, so oblivious to the idea that there was more than one universe, more than one reality, so free from concerns over this world that a person could fall asleep while watching inane and innocuous television shows.

She glanced at her phone — 10:13 pm.

Crap! She was late.

Half-falling and half-jumping out of her car, Roni scurried across the street and onto the sidewalk. Every inch of her skin tingled, shooting off nervous energy like a fireworks display. All the sounds around her amplified in her ears — her clicking footsteps, the rustle of her coat, the chirping crickets, and the hooting of an owl. Loudest of all — her breathing.

As she neared the house, her pace slowed. The outside porch light was on, bathing the front yard in yellow light. The laughter of two old ladies dribbled out from the living room. Amazing. Gram had only met Jane a few minutes ago and already the two were carrying on like old friends.

Bright lights crossed the yard as a car turned onto the street. Roni dashed forward and crouched behind an old Toyota in the driveway. The car cruised right by without indication that the driver noticed anything wrong.

Roni counted to ten, forcing a sense of calm, before scampering along the side of the house to the back. With careful, slow motions, she placed one foot on the back steps. As she increased her weight on that foot, the wooden step groaned. She waited. When nobody called out and no lights clicked on, she brought her other foot down on the next step. Another groan. Another wait. Twice more and she reached the back door.

If Gram did her job right, not only did she have Jane chatting it up in the front, but she also had managed to unlock the back door without getting caught. Roni swallowed against her tightening throat as she reached out for the doorknob. Unbelievable — it turned. Gram had done it.

Roni opened the door enough to slip inside and brought it to a close as softly as possible. Crouching in the kitchen, she listened. Jane and Gram continued to chat. Nothing to indicate Jane had heard the door open or close.

Staying low, she crept across the floor until she reached the open archway leading to a short hall and then the living room. Her thighs burned from the prolonged crouch and duck-walking — she would have to get back to doing yoga before trying this again.

She paused at that thought. Again? She had no intention of ever doing this again. Did she?

Gram's voice cut into her thoughts. "Really, Jane, it's fine. I don't need any tea."

"Nonsense," Jane said. "A delightful new friend deserves some hospitality."

Crap. Roni looked around the kitchen for a hiding place. Under the kitchen table might have been an option if it had a tablecloth large enough to cover the sides. She might have been able to contort her way into one of the lower cabinets if she had the time and flexibility. In the pantry might have been worthwhile if she didn't have to cross the entire kitchen to get there. Which left an unpleasant option.

She stood straight up, made a fist, and waited at the side of the archway. Once Jane walked into the kitchen, Roni planned to clock the lady on the head and make a run for it. Ugly and distasteful, but probably effective.

Jane's footsteps came closer. Roni had never punched anybody before. Summoning the courage she hoped resided deep within her, she pulled back her fist, ready to strike.

With an embarrassed laugh, Gram said, "Please, don't

make the tea. I appreciate the offer, but well, if I drink tea this late at night, I'll be in the bathroom for hours."

Jane halted. "Oh, I'm so sorry. I didn't even think about that."

"It's okay."

"Look at you, turning all red. There's nothing to be bashful about. If we old ladies can't be honest with each other in the privacy of our homes, then what the hell is the rest of the world going to do? Me, I've been fortunate. Got a bladder as tight and strong as if I were in my twenties. I can't boast about the rest of me — more aches and pains than I'd ever thought possible. So, forget about the tea."

"Thank you," Gram said, and Roni released a shaking breath. "You mentioned a blanket you made?"

"Oh, yes. Made it for my son a few years ago. It's up in our guest room."

"I'd love to go see it."

"Come with me."

And like that, Gram had Jane going upstairs. Hands shaking, Roni took a moment to count to ten. Once she had regained her self-control, she strode down the hall and into the living room.

She moved quickly and with purpose. Gram wouldn't be able to keep Jane up there staring at a blanket for long. Roni went straight to where Jane had kept her photo album. She pulled out a volume and flipped through the pages until she found it — the second ticket stub.

Pulling back the plastic that covered the page, Roni did not even flinch at the ripping sound. She picked the ticket stub loose, put it in her pocket, closed the photo album, and set it back from where she had snatched it. Having that tiny scrap of paper in her pocket sent warm bubbles of excitement through her blood. She had done it.

As she walked back to the kitchen, she heard Gram and

Jane clumping down the stairs. Gram hit each step with a strong thud to warn Roni, if necessary. Roni grinned as she headed out of the house.

A few minutes later, after she had crossed a few backyards and popped out on a side street, she slid into the driver's seat of her car. Almost ten minutes went by before Gram came walking toward the car. She acted casual. Just out for a night stroll.

When she got into the car, Roni wanted to tell her that everything went well. She wanted to describe how it felt to sneak around and what a good job Gram had done diverting Jane. But before Roni could utter a word, Gram pointed at the steering wheel. "You going to drive us away from your crime or are we going to sit here and wait for the cops to show up?"

Roni drove them back to the bookstore in Olburg and never said a word.

CHAPTER 19

After dropping Gram off for the night, Roni lucked into a parking space one block from her apartment and walked in the opposite direction. Two blocks later, she sidled up to a stool at Connor's Corner Bar. Near midnight and only a few customers — the heavy drinkers not willing to call it quits on a weeknight. A few of them eyed up Roni, perhaps hoping to get lucky, but thankfully, they read the situation right and returned to their drinks.

Roni ordered a shot, downed it, and ordered another. She wanted liquid fortitude to get her through the night — and only liquids from this universe. With any luck, the alcohol would provide a better sleep aid than any pills.

"You okay?" a grizzled man said from the end of the bar. He must have been near-seventy and had a beer gut to prove that he had spent most of his years in one bar or another.

"Fine," she said, though her shot spilled on her hand as she attempted to bring it to her mouth. Throwing it back, she ordered two more.

"Care to talk about it?"

She glared at him. "Do I look like I want to talk?"

Sipping a beer, he said, "No, ma'am, you do not."

"Then why are you bothering me?"

"People don't usually come to a bar like this to be alone. They come to spill their guts, sometimes their drinks, and not be judged. Or to drown their sorrows, as the saying goes. Is that why you're here? You broke up with a boyfriend or something?"

Roni swung her foot out and slipped off the stool. Her legs wobbled and the room took a short detour before lining up with her vision. Four shots in quick succession on an empty stomach — not a smart idea.

The man shook his head, and a few other men stared at her. "You all think you know what's what," she said, her words not quite crisp and clear. "You sit here in this pit and drink away, and you think you got it all under control, figured out, that you know the way the world works. Right? There are rich folk and poor folk and hard-working folk. But you're wrong. There's worlds and worlds and worlds out there. You can't ever figure it out because the rules are not set in stone. It's all in flux. One day, you're struggling to find a job and have a good, normal life, and then BAM! Next day, nothing makes sense. Pretty soon you find yourself breaking into an old lady's home to steal her memories." Roni laughed at that. "Memories. Got to steal some since I ain't got enough of my own."

The men watched her as they would the television. She certainly wasn't the first to get drunk too fast and monologue about things that made no sense. She wouldn't be the last. For them, she was the entertainment for the evening.

She thought about ordering another shot but held off. Four was already three too many. Stumbling out of the bar, she let the night air refresh her senses. With her head clearing, she weaved her way back to her apartment.

By the time she reached her door, her stomach had decided that rushing alcohol through the body might not have been such a good idea. She clamped her mouth shut, fumbled with the keys, shoved open the door, and darted to her kitchen sink. The booze burned coming up as much as it had going down. Afterwards, however, she felt better, clearer. Which only served to bring back her jumbled thoughts over what had happened that night.

It had been thrilling — if she wanted to be honest — but the way Gram spoke bothered her. So nonchalant. As if robbing people had become second nature and only a slight inconvenience to the day.

Roni guessed that dealing with rips between universes year after year jaded a person towards other matters. After all, what better justification for any crime than trying to save the universe?

She meandered into her living room. Shoving aside a pile of rumpled clothes, she made room on the couch to plop down.

"It's over," she said, her voice hollow in the late night.

At some point in the next day or two, Elliot would track down Darin. Gram and Sully would join him and together, the three of them would stop the current madness. None of that, however, involved Roni. She had done her part, and she had nothing left to offer the group.

Gram knew that all along. She knew Roni did not have magic powers like the rest of them. She knew Roni would not be casual about thievery. The whole talk of legacy and decisions meant nothing. Gram had put on that act because she knew Roni would never join.

Roni rubbed her throbbing head. Where were these thoughts coming from? She and Gram had not gotten along much lately, but Roni knew better than to think so ill of her. Yet it felt like the truth. Not in some mystical, clairvoyant way, but rather, it seemed to Roni that she could assess Gram better lately.

"Or maybe I'm still a bit drunk," she muttered.

She let her body fall to the side, her head resting on the clothes pile, and she closed her eyes. Something poked at her side. Trying to ignore it, to let sleep take over, she wiggled deeper into the clothes. But that only made the object poking her dig in more.

Sighing, she sat back up and tossed a cushion aside to find out what lay underneath. Her photo album — blue with thin lines of gold swirls. Though she knew she would grow maudlin if she looked through the book, especially half-drunk, she opened it anyway.

The simple album contained the only photographs Roni owned depicting her with her parents. Ten pictures. That was all she had.

She knew every part of the photographs. She knew the way her mother's hair curled up at the ends in the one at the beach and how her father's hand squeezed her mother's side in the one from a New Year's Eve party. But of all ten, the best one showed her mother holding baby Roni in her arms while her father gazed on mesmerized by the beauty of the ladies in his life.

The rest of the album was empty.

One blank page after another.

A thought burst forth in her head — something so strong and obvious as she thought it that she could not conceive how she had failed to think of it before. Her lack of memory, her lost time, had to be connected to Gram and the Parallel Society. It wasn't normal to lose so many years of memory — not unless there was a birth defect or a physical trauma. Mental trauma could cause amnesia but not like this. Could it?

And like that, she settled into the idea quite easily.

Tomorrow, whether Gram wanted it or not, Roni would accept her position in the Society. She would learn all she could about the Society, she would do her best job as their librarian, and she would have access to all those books. If the answer waited for her in there — and she felt more and more confident that it did — then she would find it.

Thinking about that huge room full of old journals and diaries and maps, Roni whispered, "This might take years." That did not sit well. The idea of spending so much time wrapped up in the Society that she might end up like the Old Gang churned her stomach — or was it the alcohol?

But would it be so bad to spend that time in the bookstore? She would be able to learn all about the other worlds. She would get chances to help people like Darin, and in the future, she would be able to help them the right way instead of this mess they were cleaning up. And with some more honesty in her heart, she admitted she had nowhere else to go. At least, the Society would give her a reason to get out of the apartment in the morning.

She closed her eyes and sunk her head back into the clothes pile. Tomorrow morning. She would deal with these questions tomorrow morning.

CHAPTER 20

The phone rang. Roni jolted awake, her head foggy as she scanned the room — her apartment. At least she made it home safe — she checked around the room again — and alone.

Picking up the phone, she licked the film from her teeth. "Morning."

"Elliot found your boyfriend," Gram said.

Roni held the phone away from her ear and turned the volume down. "Okay. Thanks for letting me know."

"Are you not listening? We know where Darin is. It's time to get to work."

After a pause, Roni realized that Gram waited for her to say something. "Good luck."

"Don't you want to know where Darin is? How else do you plan to find the place?"

That woke up Roni's brain. "Why would I have to be there? I did my part. I got the ticket stub. There's nothing else for me to do except leave the rest in the hands of those with powers."

"Having powers doesn't mean ... oh, never mind. Darin is holed up in an abandoned house bordering Kaneslow

Cemetery. You know where Kaneslow is?"

"Near Reading."

"Right. Should take you about thirty, forty-five minutes to get there. On the left side of First Street as you come in from the south, you'll see a diner. We'll meet you there."

"But what can I do except get in the way?"

She could hear Gram's disapproving breaths. "You made me a promise that you would see this to the end. Well, it isn't over until Darin is dealt with. Are you a woman of her word or not?"

"Oh, for crying out loud. Does everything have to be a measure of my worth to you?" She couldn't believe the words had come out of her mouth. From the long pause, Gram apparently had the same shock.

At length, in a stoic tone, Gram said, "The thing that has taken over Darin may end up being all bark and no bite. I've seen it before. They all boast that this world is ripe for the plucking and they'll be the ones to take it. Sometimes they are a serious threat. Sometimes they're nothing but talkers. But sometimes, and I fear this is the case with Darin, they are more like an invasive species of plant. They're like kudzu. They come in and their mere presence starts to effect the surrounding area. They multiply and pretty soon, your world doesn't look like it once did. They seem harmless but they can be the worst of all."

"Okay, okay. No need for a full-on lecture. You want me there, I'll be there. Okay?"

"Elliot's the one insisting you come along."

"Jeez, I'm just waking up. I'll meet you at the diner as soon as I can."

Without waiting for a response, Roni ended the call. She brushed her teeth, splashed water on her face, and dug a few semi-clean clothes from the pile she had slept on. Then she checked her phone to find the fastest route to the diner, and off she went.

The drive offered no troubles other than her splitting headache. She had downed a couple of ibuprofen but either they had not kicked in fast enough or she needed more.

The town of Kaneslow looked like many Pennsylvania towns — a steady mixture of modern homes and stores with buildings from the original colonial settlements. Sprinkled in between were modern homes done in a colonial style.

She parked outside the diner — affectionately called the First Street Diner. Inside, she found Gram and Elliot at a booth near the back. Elliot had a plate with the remnants of eggs, toast, sausage patties, and hash browns. Gram had a cup of coffee.

"Where's Sully?" Roni asked as she slid in next to Elliot.

"He'll be here," Gram said. "He never lets us down."

Roni couldn't tell if Gram meant the comment as a fact or a slight. She opened her mouth to set things straight before they got any further, but Elliot spoke up.

"Let me tell you what I know so far. Sully won't care about most of this, and since he will probably stay in the back, he has no need for these details."

Gram nodded. "He's always been good at improvising, anyway."

"And he likes it that way. Makes it more exciting."

A brief grin. "It does fill him with life, doesn't it? Okay. Tell us what you've got."

Leaning in on his elbows, he lowered his voice. The conspiratorial nature of the move woke Roni more, sending an excited tingle across her skin. "On the other side of town, they have three churches all next to each other. Each one has a cemetery, and as far as I can tell, the land bleeds one into the other, so it's really like one enormous cemetery. In the woods surrounding the cemetery, there is an abandoned house.

"Now, that place has been here long enough to have built up some bits of legend around it. As far as I could learn chatting with the locals, it once belonged to the Stoltz family — husband, wife, and a little girl. All those acres of cemetery were the Stoltz farm.

"Apparently, Mr. Stoltz was quite a respectable man. Church-goer, stern and fair, and a hard worker. All good attributes in the 1700s. But something went wrong. Nobody saw it coming. There was no build up, no slow change in behavior. Just one night, he snapped. Killed his wife and his child while they slept. Slit their throats, then shot himself."

Taking a sip of coffee, Gram said, "You thinking Darin chose that place because of its energy?"

"Possibly."

"Energy?" Roni said. "Like auras and stuff?"

"Nonsense," Gram said. "Elliot is suggesting that there might have been a universe tear in the house. If Mr. Stoltz stumbled upon it and got infected by it — much like Darin, except this would have been by accident — then that would explain the sudden shift in personality and behavior. Either he was taken over like Darin, or more likely, contact with another universe drove him mad."

Elliot said, "It might still be going on, too. The legends I heard all suggest the house is haunted. Brave and stupid kids try to spend the night there but never make it. A few were never seen again. Those kinds of stories."

"Hold on," Roni said, her brain playing catch-up with the words her ears relayed. "Are you telling me that all those haunted house tales you hear growing up, that those are really people getting caught up with rips between universes?"

"Sometimes. Most times, really. In this case, I see all the

hallmarks of a universe tear. Plus, it would explain why Darin zeroed in on the place. Because that's where he is."

"I don't get it. Why would he hide like a criminal on the run? He left us all full of himself and ready to take over the world."

Gram tapped one finger on the table. "Remember what I said? Some of these beings are all bluster. Maybe that's the case with him."

"No," Elliot said. "This one is dangerous. Maybe not *take over the world* dangerous, but he's got some serious strength and anger. I think that move he did at the zoo, transforming himself with those wolves, that must have taken a lot out of him. He's not hiding in that farmhouse so much as healing. And when he is ready, he will strike again."

The waitress finally noticed Roni had joined the table. She slapped a menu down, poured coffee, and walked off. Roni pushed the menu aside. The greasy aroma of all the food around her was bad enough, the thought of eating food threatened to send her running to the bathroom.

Frowning, she asked, "Why would he be attracted to this tear? It's not his universe. Is it? Can there be more than one tear into the same universe?"

"Good questions," Elliot said. "The answer will not be so good. Basically, we do not know. We think it might be possible for there to be more than one tear, but we have never seen it. We have seen that oftentimes beings are attracted to the tears themselves, but we've never put it to a test, so we cannot say definitively."

Gram added, "The Society doesn't have the time or resources to conduct deep investigations on these kinds of questions. It's one of the big drawbacks to keeping the group so small. The answers might be in our library of journals and such, but well, you've seen that room. Perhaps such questions will be answered by those who take up the call after us. Not really your concern though, since you'll be leaving after this is done."

Sully arrived in time to prevent Roni from snapping a response. He shuffled his feet as he approached, his face unshaven and his remaining hair sticking out at odd angles. He slumped into the booth with a hiss and a wince.

"You okay?" Roni asked.

"Just my back," he said. "When you get as old as me, see how well you do." The waitress came by right away this time. "Bagel, toasted, with a shmeer on the side."

Gram rolled her beaded necklace between two fingers and inspected Sully closely. Her face turned livid. "Are you serious?"

"What?" He looked to Roni. "What's she on about?"

"Don't pretend you don't know what you did. Is this really how you want Roni to see this group function? After all our years of hard work, is this really what you think we should be doing now? Screwing things up like this?"

"You know who's screwing this up? The waitress. She never poured me any coffee."

"You didn't ask for any, and don't change the subject."

Roni pushed her coffee across the table. "Will someone tell me what's going on?"

Gram arched an eyebrow at Sully, but when it became clear he wouldn't open up, she said, "This genius was supposed to be in his workshop —"

"I was in my workshop."

"— making a new Golem for today. Instead, he fell asleep."

Stabbing the air with his finger, Sully said, "First, I didn't have the clay to make it. I used up most of what I had to make the one a few days ago. You all think I'm some magic wizard that can create supplies from thin air. No. I need more clay. Second, I've been telling you the wiring in my workshop is bad. Not enough power for what I need. So, I had troubles there. Third, I am an old man and I need rest to do good work. Should a doctor be so tired he falls asleep in surgery? Should a pilot skip a nap and crash a plane? The work we do is more important than those, so yes, I went to sleep. Look at the bags under your eyes and Roni, too. You both could use a few more hours rest."

"Never you mind Roni and me. We're here, on time, and ready to do our jobs. But I guess we won't have a Golem to back us up in case there's trouble. And when isn't there trouble?"

Elliot broke in. "Stop it. Both of you. Sully, from now on, please keep us informed when it comes to your clay orders. We could have purchased more last month easily. Lillian, we will be fine without a big Golem. I have the fullest confidence that Sully can still be an asset. Besides, with any luck, it won't matter because Roni is going to talk Darin in."

Sputtering, Roni said, "I am? No, no, no. That's not a good idea."

Putting up his hand to quell any further protests, Elliot remained calm. The waitress arrived with Sully's food, and they all sat quiet until she left. Gram shifted forward with a clear intention to speak her mind, but Elliot raised his hand again.

"Let me speak," he said, and Gram sat back. "There are many reasons this is a good idea. We have several concerns to deal with in this situation. Obviously, we wish to return this creature from whence it came, save Darin's life, and close any other tears we might find. But more important than all of those things, we must protect the people of this town from exposure to all of this." To Roni, he added, "Sometimes we are lucky and our cases take us into remote parts of the world where we can act freely, but more often, we are in situations such as this one. Plenty of people attend those churches and visit those cemeteries. If we have Roni talk with Darin, if she is successful, we can achieve all of our goals without causing any contamination of the townsfolk."

Gram shook her head. "Roni's never done anything like this."

"We all began as such."

"But she doesn't know the first thing —"

"She is the only one of us with a connection to the victim. That is why the wolf creature Darin offered to have her join him. Somewhere inside, there is a tiny spark of the original Darin left. It is why we acquired the second ticket stub, and it is why I think Roni will succeed."

Roni said, "I think Gram's right. I don't know what I could possibly say to him that would make him give up. What could anybody say?"

"If you're going to be part of this Society, you will have to take risks. You will have to dig deep into your soul to find those words you need."

"Well, you said it right there." Gram lifted her chin. "Roni has no intention of being one of us. We couldn't have put a more welcoming embrace, considering the situation, yet she hems-and-haws, unsure of herself, unwilling to commit. This is not the kind of person we want in the Society."

Elliot thumped his cane on the floor garnering a few surreptitious glances from other diners. "If your granddaughter does not even try —"

"She's made her decision."

"I have not," Roni said with enough force to quiet everyone at the table. Even Sully looked up at her in surprise. "You all seem to think I should be acclimating far quicker than I am. I'm sorry about that, but that's the way it is. I didn't get eased into this. Perhaps if, while I was growing up, Gram had prepared me for this Society and all that it entails or, at the least, given me a hint that things might not be the way I thought they were, well, then maybe I'd be able to decide faster."

Elliot took hold of Roni's hand. "I'm sure it has been quite difficult for you. I wish we had the time to do all of this right. Sully and I have wanted to tell you the truth for years, but your grandmother kept saying you weren't ready."

"That's not true," Gram said. "I never said that she wasn't ready. I said that I didn't want to burden her with our responsibilities." To Roni, she added, "You've had an unfortunate childhood and you've been aimless for a long time. I didn't think you needed to be bothered with all of this. Look at you — caught with this big decision which will impact the rest of your life, yet no time to think about it because we've got Darin Lander to deal with. This was what I wanted to avoid."

"There is no avoiding. Sully and I told you as much more than enough times."

Roni knew she would be unpacking all that she had heard for days, but at the moment, Darin needed help. "Is there another plan that doesn't involve me lying to Darin?"

Elliot said, "You do not have to lie to him. I never said such a thing. But you are the one who must talk to him."

"I just don't think —"

"You must try. If you do not, we might perish. Not just me or Sully or your grandmother, but all of us. Whether on purpose or by accident, this version of Darin has the potential to destroy the world as we know it. Not overnight, of course — at least, I hope not — but as time goes by. Maybe months, maybe a few years. Who knows?

Right now, though, this is the only opportunity we will get to stamp out this trouble before it truly begins."

Roni knew she had no real choice. Part of her knew it all along. "Fine. I'll try. When do we begin?"

"Right away."

"Hold on, hold on." Sully put a hand on his plate. "I still have my bagel to finish."

CHAPTER 21

As they drove to the cemetery, all four in Elliot's Lincoln, Roni could not stop her knees from bouncing or her fingers from tapping. Her nerves firing off reminded her of sitting for a final exam in college — one that she had not prepared for. Strange. She could remember a sensation like that even when she could barely remember the faces, names, and events of her past. It had never bothered her much, this lost time, but now she found herself thinking about it more than ever.

"Just ahead," Elliot said.

He drove under an iron gate with the words Kaneslow Cemetery on the arch. A gravel driveway led to a small parking lot. A red Subaru Outback sat at the end of the lot. As they got out of the Lincoln, Roni spotted three men standing by a grave — an elderly man, a younger man and a boy.

The morning sun rose high enough to cast shadows off the gravestones, and Roni's skin chilled. They were more than shadows. They marked other lives — people and families and histories she would never know. Each one like a universe unto itself. Each one a book in the cavern.

"Come," Elliot said, and Roni shook off her dark thoughts.

He led the way along a white stone path. After a short distance, they crested a hill and soon they could no longer see the cars or the three men by the grave. Roni wanted to rush ahead even as she wanted to rush back to the car, but neither would do. The Old Gang moved at a slow and steady pace, and she would have to get comfortable with it. No way could she manage this alone.

Up ahead, she saw a thick tree line — the beginning of a forest that wound its way around several towns and eventually connected with Norris Acres Park. Just inside the tree line, a silhouette of a farmhouse partially hid. A one-floor rancher, small, probably a single room with bed, stove, and table all smack up next to each other. Practical for a farmer centuries ago.

The closer they walked, the more the house struck Roni as a dead and rotting beast. The windows were cracked or missing. The wood had split in some places, been eaten by insects, and hollowed out in others.

When they reached the tree line, Elliot halted and pointed at the ground. "Blood."

Roni had to crouch down and squint to view the two spots Elliot had indicated. They definitely were there, but without touching them, she had no way to know if they were fresh. She didn't really want to know, either.

They entered the woods. The leaves shushed as the wind blew through — a thousand librarians angry at their trespass. Sunlight speckled the ground but not enough to warm the air. The temperature must have dropped five degrees, maybe more.

Many of the trees surrounding the house had been removed to create some space but not all of them. Shadows covered the area well enough. As they stepped towards the front of the house, Roni noticed she could barely see the cemetery.

Gram swung her big bag over her shoulder as she looked at the building. "Sully, get to work."

Roni expected his usual sass, but instead, he nodded and walked deeper into the woods. The seriousness in his steps, in the way he focused on the ground, in the fearful glance shot back at the house, spiked Roni's heart rate. She wanted to throw up.

"You are going to do fine," Elliot said, nudging her shoulder. "Just talk with him."

A wood porch large enough for two rocking chairs with an overhang had been built up to the front door. The warped wood looked like subtle waves on calm waters. But Roni knew better, now. Nothing calm awaited her. Vicious monsters swam the waters ahead, ready to strike.

She stepped forward.

"Darin?" Her voice sounded tiny in the forest. She cleared her throat. "Darin?" More forceful this time, but it still felt small. "I came here to talk. That's all. I want to make sure you're okay. I want to help you figure this out. For everyone's sake."

Sully returned with a mass of sticks cradled in his arms. He set them on the ground in a haphazard pile and walked off again.

Chiding herself to stay focused, Roni said, "Please, come out and talk with me. You know we're not going to leave. This isn't about how you're going to beat us. It's about how this will end. I should be angrier than ever with you, but I'm not. I only want to talk, to help, to make this better. That's it."

Nothing. Not a sound.

Roni glanced back at Elliot and shrugged. He offered a consolatory nod — she tried. Lifting his cane over his head with one hand, he began circling the air in front of him with the other.

But a loud squeaking broke the silence. The front door opened inward.

Elliot lowered his cane. He and Gram stepped up on either side of Roni. Through the open door, they could see nothing more than darkness. They walked ahead together until they reached the steps onto the porch.

Darin's deep voice boomed out. "Just Roni."

Roni put her foot on the first step, but Gram's hand shot out. Clenching Roni's arm, she said, "Don't go in there."

"Why am I out here then?"

"This isn't a game. There is real danger inside that house. I know we don't get along that well lately, but I don't want to see you hurt."

"I have to try." Roni's confidence began and ended with those words. As she climbed onto the porch, her heart sank into her gut, her chin quivered, and her mouth went bone dry. Like a painted line leading into the house, Roni saw dark blood — something had been dragged across the wood. Barely above a whisper, she repeated, "I have to try."

Her stomach gurgled and a burning sensation coursed through her lower abdomen. She kept her mouth a thin line and focused on not flinching from the discomfort. Part of Darin had been changed into a wolf, and Roni knew that with animals, particularly dogs, she had to show as little fear as possible.

Crossing the threshold into the house, she fought to remain still. A putrid, rotting odor threatened to knock her down. Her legs wobbled, desperate to whip her around and sprint off into the woods.

The glow of low coals from a once hearty fire burned in the hearth. A plain, wood table had been placed a few feet away. On that table, Roni saw the body of a man — split open, his innards hanging off the side. Next to the body, she saw the head of a fawn. In the back corner, Darin sat in the dark.

"I thought it would be easier," he said. "Apparently, merging with the wolf was a one-time experience. Back home, we merge and depart without thought. We take the best we can from each other and attempt to give off the worst. Some of us can even force two others to converge on a point." He gestured to the table. "It doesn't work in this world."

Roni shifted so that she faced Darin fully and could not see any of the horror on the table. Breathing through her mouth to avoid smelling the severed stomach, she said, "No matter how many times you try, it won't ever work. Our worlds are too different."

"But I'm here. I'm fine. And it worked for me."

"Like you said — a one-time thing."

"Unless I can figure out a way to change that. I have time, and I'm sure I can find your most intelligent people."

"Why would they help you?"

"They won't have a choice. I can think of countless ways to threaten them, their families, anyone they love."

"Or you could admit what you know is the truth. That this world isn't right for you. That you should go back to your home."

Darin jumped to his feet, his wolf mouth snarling. "When I was young — a boy, you would call me — I was little more than the size of a thumb. Just a glowing ball of energy. I'd bounce around, merge with other young ones, and I stupidly believed I had been born into a beautiful world. But my mother, for lack of a better word, she wanted me to be something I was not. She cared about that kind of thing. She would chase me around, watch every move, every decision, every aspect of my life. It got to the point where I found it difficult to function. So, I left. And I don't have the time or interest to explain how my world works, but suffice it to say, I did not excel."

"Most people don't — at least, not in the way we think we should."

"I mean something different. But while I had no hope of achieving the higher planes — and don't bother asking — I did learn to take better aspects of a merge and discard the worst. I could fight off multiple threats, and I knew some of the best places to rest, heal, and prepare for the next outing.

"I also started to work. My mother kept tabs on me still and I knew she would be disappointed when she saw to what lows I had achieved. It gave me the only happiness I ever had — watching her fall apart because of me."

Roni inched back toward the door. She needed fresh air. "Your mother won't see anything you do here."

He moved towards her. Blood had splattered across his clothes and speckled the fur on his neck. "What you just said is the biggest problem I have."

"Then go back. She's there. Waiting to be humiliated by you."

"You don't understand." He looked pained and frustrated. At least, Roni thought that was how he looked — she never had to read a wolf's facial cues before. Darin's yellow wolf-eyes narrowed as if he struggled to force out the words. "I have no mother."

"But you just said —"

"That wasn't my mother. That was Darin's mother. We — my species — we do not have mothers and fathers. We split and reform. Do you see now? Darin and I are blending in a way that shouldn't happen. I can't tell where my life ends and his begins. We are one being now."

"What about the wolf? He in there, too?"

"The wolf cannot think at a high enough level to merge our thoughts that way. So, now you understand. Now, you must leave."

Roni edged back further. "You know I can't do that. I'm here because you can't continue like this. I'm here because that man you are part of, Darin, he doesn't deserve this."

Darin bent closer, his canine breath hot and foul. "There's no point in trying to save him. We are entwined. There is no going back."

She tried to hold her ground, but her legs stepped toward the door anyway. "I know it's not the same, but lately, I've felt like I had two people entwined within me. One wants desperately to forget all of this ever happened. One wants to embrace it all, jump off into the excitement of it. It can drive you to do dumb things, erratic things. But it doesn't have to be bad. I'm sure there are ways we can gain control over our competing selves. Maybe we can help each other figure it out."

"That's your solution? You think we can talk our way through the problem and find some happy balance that still involves me taking control of your world?"

"That's not happening, and you know it." She pointed to the table without looking at it. "This isn't going to change. We can't be merged like that."

A creak of wood on the porch caused Roni and Darin to freeze. He cocked his head as his wolf ears perked up. He snatched a glance at the back window. A Gram-shaped figured darted by.

"I see," Darin said with a low growl. "You don't mean anything you are saying. You've only been stalling."

"No," Roni said. "I don't know what they're up to, but I had nothing to do with it. I was sent in here to talk with you, to try to find a peaceful solution."

"Liar." His lips lifted to reveal his long fangs. Saliva dribbled down through the fur on his face and onto the floor. "You are a stupid, insignificant, worthless piece of meat. That's the truth you must learn. You are nothing but food to me."

"So now you're all wolf and going to start eating people? What happened to changing us all?" Roni's hands trembled at her side. She felt the warped porch underneath her as she continued backing up. She had no clue what words tumbled out of her mouth, but she figured as long as they were speaking to each other, he wasn't killing her — that seemed like a good choice.

"You disgust me. You pretend to care about Darin or me or us, but you're nothing but a manipulator."

With a bark, he jumped forward forcing her back. Her foot reached the end and missed the stairs. Flailing her arms, Roni smacked into the earth. She scrambled to her feet and dashed for Elliot.

Darin towered at the edge of the porch. Muscles he never had a few nights before now bulged through his shirt. His fingernails had thickened and grown longer.

Roni stood behind Elliot. He leaned on his cane and watched. His old, stained shirt made him appear scrawny. What had she been thinking? How could these three people — so old they were ready to sit in wheelchairs at a retirement home — how could they be the saviors of all? Sure, Roni had seen them in action before, but not like this. Not against a beast like Darin.

It was one thing to prepare for a fight on home turf with special rings in the walls and magic forces ready at hand. Even then, they had narrowly survived. But this — this creature outclassed them. Roni was the only one of the Society who could move with any sure speed, and she had no doubt that Darin could chase her down without getting winded.

"I shall give you one chance," Elliot said — even his accented voice sounded weak. "Come with us peacefully, and all will be fine."

Darin barked twice as his answer. Then he inhaled hard, his chest widening as it filled up, and let loose a long howl. By the time the single note faded, four wolves entered from deeper in the woods. They snapped their jaws, growled, and barked.

Roni felt urine trickle down her leg. "We're going to die."

CHAPTER 22

Elliot patted Roni's arm. "I shall take care of this," he said. "You go help Sully."

"But —"

"Go." His voice suddenly firm and dangerous. He stepped closer to the porch, letting the wolves flank him. Pointing at Darin with his cane like Babe Ruth showing where he would hit the next homerun, Elliot said, "I do not wish to harm you. Heel your wolves now. There will be no more chances after this."

Darin paused, and Roni had the time to think that maybe he had changed his mind. But a swipe of his claw through the air sent the wolves into a frenzied attack. Roni backed away, her eyes stuck wide open, as she witnessed Elliot's incredible reaction.

The first wolf thrust into the air, and Elliot ducked, jabbing his cane upward to catch the wolf's gut as it passed overhead. Two more came in from the sides. A sweeping motion of the cane halted their approach. The fourth barreled in full-speed with its teeth bared. As Elliot finished his sweep, he let his momentum carry him to the ground. He rolled backwards and onto his feet. This gave him plenty of distance to swing his cane hard enough to crack the attacking wolf's skull.

"Roni!" a voice called from behind. She spun around to find Sully with another armful of sticks. "Yes, yes, he's amazing. But at his age, he won't keep that up for long. He's counting on us to finish this. Come. Help."

Behind her, she heard the grunts and smacks and growls turn to bites, but she pushed it from her mind. She had to help Sully.

"What do we do?" she asked looking at the pile of sticks.

"Find the big ones." He grabbed a thick branch and drew lines in the dirt. "Two legs here. Arms here. Body and head. Put the biggest branches first, then put on all the sticks. Then tie them together."

"Right. Big sticks, little sticks, tie it all together. Wait — tie them with what?"

Sully reached into his coat pocket and tossed out a handful of zip-ties. "Hurry."

As she picked up the ties, she snatched a glimpse of Elliot. With one wolf dead on the ground, the other three increased the pressure. One after the other, sometimes two together, even all three. Attack after attack. And Elliot fended them off with a swirling cane and a well-trained fist.

Roni grabbed the biggest branches she saw and placed them on the ground. Frantically, she spread the smaller sticks all over the skeletal form.

"No, no," Sully said. "That's a mess. That won't do. Do it right or we'll lose whatever time Elliot buys us."

Moving fast, Roni picked up the sticks and laid them into the proper positions. Blood dribbled on her hand from the numerous cuts she received but she kept going. Elliot cried out and she saw him deflect one wolf with his cane while clutching another by the neck. The third, however, bit into Elliot's calf.

Roni doubled her efforts. As she worked, Sully sat on the ground with a pad and pen. She knew he would be writing in Hebrew, that she wouldn't be able to read it, but she wanted to watch him. No — she had to finish the stick-Golem.

With the zip-ties, she gathered up each limb and tied them into bundles. When she finished, sweat and blood mixed in her palms. "Is this good?"

Sully scowled. "No."

"What's wrong? The legs and arms and body are all tied up."

"But not together. The legs aren't attached."

"I didn't know."

"What are you thinking? How's it going to walk without attached legs?"

"I'll fix it."

Sully peeked up at Elliot and shook his head. "Not enough time."

Elliot had maimed a second wolf, but the two remaining sensed his flagging energy. They stalked closer, and though he swiped with his cane, they barely flinched. Sweat dampened his head. His footprints left behind splotches of blood.

Darin laughed — a full-throated barking laugh. "You're pathetic. Far past your prime. If you're what I have to worry about, then once I fix the merging process, this world will crumble."

Two metal chains with spiked ends whipped around the corner of the building and lodged into Darin's back. Gram leaned away from the porch, putting all her weight into holding Darin still. He bellowed and the two wolves on Elliot pivoted away. But Elliot lunged forward, tackling both — one with his body, the other with his cane.

"Roni!" Gram's voice strained to be heard over Darin's howling cries. "Roni, help us!"

Having no idea how to help, Roni rushed forward anyway. She kept a wide berth around the wolves. Elliot used his weight and the last of the strength to keep the animals locked to the ground.

Darin swiped a claw in Roni's direction, but another chain shot out and wrapped around his wrist. Gram yanked that wrist back.

And Roni saw it — Darin's stomach. A flicker of amber light.

That had to be it. She knew it like an instinct. But no, if the answer were that simple, surely Gram would have said something, would have known. She shoved the idea away.

But it refused to leave. And in that second, the idea took her by the chest and shook her inside. It yelled at her that she had ignored her instincts too often and where did that ever get her? If she had listened in the beginning, she would have gotten rid of Darin from the start.

Well, nothing else is working, she thought.

Storming up the steps of the porch, she made a fist and punched. She yelled, her face inches away from Darin's snout, her eyes manic and wide. Her fist hit him in the gut, and as she had guessed, it kept going — straight through and into his abdomen.

Darin roared. He tried to grab her or push her, but Gram kept him restrained. Roni plunged her hand further in, holding back the urge to vomit, until she hit something pulsing hot. At first, she thought it might be his heart — maybe his innards had reshaped along with his outward appearance. But no, she knew what she grasped onto. It could only be one thing.

She yanked her arm free, causing another howling shriek, and staggered off the porch. Blood and bile dripped from her forearm, the smell ripe and vulgar. In her palm, she held the glowing ball.

All eyes lifted to her. The wolves ceased their struggle and watched her every move. Elliot stared in shock. Even as Gram held Darin back, her attention fell on Roni.

But Roni turned her focus on the glob in her hand. Something rested inside it. A small, rectangular object. Roni's face dropped open. "Oh, man."

She threw the glowing energy onto the ground. It splattered like a ball of paint. Darin screamed and tried to intervene, but moving forward meant tearing his back to pieces.

Roni crouched down. On the ground, she saw the ticket stub — Darin's ticket stub.

"No!" Darin lunged forward.

His skin tore and blood shot out his back as he freed himself. Gram fell over, her chains dropping to the ground. The wolves jumped hard, taking Elliot by surprise. He couldn't hold them back as they raced to join Darin.

Roni bent down and snatched the ticket stub before bolting off around the house. She wouldn't get far. She knew it. But she had to try. If she survived this, that would have to become her mantra — try, try, try.

Cutting around the corner of the house, she didn't dare look back. She could hear how close they were. If she darted into the woods, Darin and the wolves would get her easily. Another corner and she came up the side of the house. Whatever backup plans Gram and the others had waiting, Roni hoped they were ready.

She turned the last corner and saw Gram standing near the porch stairs. In front of her like a shield, she held a book. No, Roni realized — *the book*. The book that Darin had fallen into originally.

"Throw it!" Gram said.

Roni tossed the ticket stub into the air and kept running. As she zipped by Gram, she saw the book being opened. She dove to the ground, scrambling for the nearest tree, and wrapped her arms around its trunk.

When she looked back, she saw the two wolves spinning in the air as the book vacuumed them in. The ticket stub had already fallen into the book as did numerous leaves and rocks. Though Roni felt the strong winds, she did not have to fight to keep her position. They were in a large, open forest and Gram had pointed the book away from them. Roni was safe behind the book.

Darin, however, had to fight to stay in this universe. He dug his claws into the ground and moaned as he climbed his way back towards the house. Once close enough, he bit down on the porch railing.

After a few moments, Roni could see that Darin had secured himself well. The book would not be taking him back. Gram must have come to the same conclusion. She closed the book.

All went quiet.

CHAPTER 23

For several minutes, nobody moved. Roni's pulse beat against her neck and her heavy breathing matched that of the Old Gang. Elliot had managed to get to his feet but he leaned hard on his cane. Gram held the book to her chest and closed her eyes. Roni couldn't be sure if she prayed or simply needed rest or both.

Crumpled on the ground by the porch, Darin whimpered. His wolf hair fell out in clumps. His snout receded back into his head.

"Is that it?" Roni said, her voice cutting into the silence like a car backfiring during a church service. "Did we save him?"

Gram opened her eyes and looked over Darin. "Perhaps. Elliot?"

Dabbing at a cut on his forehead, he said, "I suspect the creature attached itself to the ticket stub. It was the man's emotional core, and thus, it became the core of the creature — its heart. By ripping the ticket stub out, Roni essentially ripped out the heart of the beast."

"So, it's over?" Roni asked.

Gram watched every motion Darin made as she

approached him. "Darin? Are you okay? How do you feel?"

His shoulders shook, but when she reached out to touch him, he whirled around with a maniacal grin on his face. "I feel damn good."

His arm circled over Gram's elbow, locking her against him. With his free hand, he slapped Gram upside the head. Dazed from the blow, she could not stop him when he plucked the book from her weakened hands.

Elliot lifted his cane and started a circle with his hand, but Roni knew there wasn't enough time for that. Though feeling spent of all her strength, she charged. Darin shoved her aside as he stepped forward. She flopped onto the ground next to Gram.

To Elliot, Darin said, "You're not so bright. The ticket stub was not the heart of me. It was the heart of old Darin." Turning back to face Roni, he laughed. "You threw away the man you wanted to save. And now I have this book, this door into my old homeworld. I have to thank you all. With this, I don't have to bother experimenting on ways to merge beings. I can simply open this and bring in my own kind."

Gram threw out a chain but Darin sidestepped the attack. His fingers slid along the book's cover, tracing the corners with affection. Roni saw it in the man's eyes — he was going to open the book and point it at them.

She had nothing to grab onto. If she ran for a tree, he would open the book long before she got there. The porch was too far away. Her only option would be to grab Gram's leg, but after all the energy they had spent to get this far, she didn't think Gram would be able to hold onto anything long enough to save them.

Roni tried not to think of that horrible Hell tunnel of flesh and faces she had seen before. Trying not think of it only made the image stronger in her mind.

"Goodbye," Darin said.

But he never got the cover open. Two arms made of sticks and branches rose behind him. The stick-Golem stood a foot taller than Darin as it locked him in a thorny bear hug.

Thrashing his legs, Darin tried to break the Golem apart. He wriggled his shoulder and thrust his head back into the mass of branches. Bits of wood spit off into the air, but the Golem did not release him.

Roni helped Gram to her feet. She trembled out a smile, but Gram shook her head. Darin had not given up yet.

As Sully walked around the scene to reach Gram, Darin pushed off the ground, stomped on the Golem's feet, and bit at the twigs near his mouth. His exertions only fueled his rage. Holding the book tight in his arms, Darin took a different tactic — he dropped. He lifted his legs off the ground and let all of his weight carry him down.

The Golem's arms and back could not move fast enough to accommodate the sudden shift in weight distribution. Two loud snaps of wood and Darin hit the dirt — free. He popped to his feet, spun around to face the Golem, and opened the book.

With splintering cracks, the broken arms of the Golem tore free of its body and soared into the suction of the book. The Golem's feet rooted into the ground, keeping the rest of it safe. Darin closed the book.

"I'm leaving here," Darin said with his back to the group. "If any of you try to stop me, I'll open the book, and you will find out how hard it is to live in another world."

He walked by the Golem, sneered at it, and kept going. Roni looked to the Old Gang for some sign of what to do, but they watched him go. They were motionless and exhausted.

"Well, I'm not giving up," she said. Digging in her pocket, she pulled out the second ticket stub. "Darin! If there's any part of you still in there, you'll want this."

He stopped.

"Can you feel it? Your father's ticket stub."

He whirled back. "How did you get that?"

"You *are* in there, aren't you? The creature in you said I threw you away, but I didn't believe it. Not entirely. If it were so easy, he would have done it long ago."

"Shut up," Darin said, but Roni thought he said it to himself. He smacked the side of his head. "Shut up. I'm in control."

"Come here, Darin. Come get your father's ticket stub. You remember that day, right? One of the best of your life."

Darin took three quick steps and halted. He stood to the side of the stick-Golem and leaned in. To Roni, he looked like a man lured by a Siren call while another, invisible man attempted to hold him back.

He stuttered another two steps and reached out. "My dad's ticket." Then he struck himself on the cheek. "Your father is dead and I am all that matters to you now."

She waved the ticket back and forth. "Courtside seats at a 76ers game. Remember? Your mother and father were proud of you and wanted to celebrate. They couldn't afford tickets for all three of you, so you had dinner together. Then just you and your father went to the game."

Darin staggered closer. She had no idea what to do once he arrived. She need not have worried.

Sully crossed his arms with one hand on each shoulder. He closed his eyes and recited Hebrew while bowing three times. What remained of the stick-Golem sprang into action. Keeping one foot with its roots held in the earth, the Golem locked its other leg around Darin's waist. It moved faster than before, and Darin had no time to react.

Elliot hobbled to Roni as fast as his injured feet would take him. "Come," he said, taking her by the hand. They scurried off to the tree line and waited.

Gram stepped before Darin. She opened her big bag and pulled out another book. "It didn't have to be this way," she said.

He spit at her. "Of course, it did."

She opened the book.

No wind. No whoosh of air. No vacuum pulled at everything in sight. And from the tree line, Roni saw only cold darkness inside.

Darin opened his eyes. He looked at Gram and then the book. As it dawned on him that he would not be sucked into oblivion, a smile crept up his mouth.

"A dud?" he said. "Your book is a dud. It didn't work! Ha!"

Gram's eyes narrowed and her voice chilled. "Not all universes are the same."

A gray and black marbled, seven fingered hand burst forth from the book. It stretched across the area on an elongated arm with multiple joints. Boils and open wounds covered the bizarre appendage.

The hand opened wide enough to encompass Darin's entire head. He screamed — a muffled sound under the palm of the hand. It pulled him back, breaking through the stick-Golem without effort.

Darin managed to get his feet under him and attempted to run off, but the hand shoved his head to the ground. He bawled in pain and fear. He kicked and yelled. As the mottle-skinned hand dragged him across the dirt and stone, he let loose a long howl that lacked all the strength of the wolf. Clutching his book, he continued to squirm on the ground.

If he thought to open the book, he failed to act on it. Not that it would have mattered. The seven-fingered hand never ceased retracting.

In seconds, it drew him down into the book Gram held. She closed it and shook her head.

CHAPTER 24

Hours later, as midnight approached, Gram led Roni, Elliot, and Sully through the twisting maze of the caverns. They stepped off the main path and went up a short incline until she finally halted by a wall with two chains hanging loose.

"Everyone doing okay?" she asked.

Elliot had spent the car ride home healing himself and then Sully. Roni said she did not require his aid. Though she did have a few bruises, she thought it would be better to avoid getting reliant on the old man.

From her bag, Gram pulled out the book that had captured Darin. It had green vertical lines down the front and wide black spaces between. She reached for the chains, paused, and lowered her arms.

Turning to Roni, she said, "This is your victory. You do the honors."

Victory. Roni didn't know if she agreed with that word. They had won, yet they failed to save Darin. Gram told her that Darin had died the moment he entered the book the first time, but that did not relieve her uneasiness.

Still, they had saved their world and their universe, so

she recognized that much of a victory. Taking the book, she moved in close to the wall. She reached up for the first chain. At her touch, it snaked down and locked itself around the book. When she brushed the other chain with her finger, it too wrapped around the book and then punctured the spine with its sharp end.

Gram motioned in the air, and both chains tightened up, securing the book against the cavern wall. The Old Gang clapped their hands and Roni blushed.

"Speech! Speech!" Sully said.

Roni knew she could not avoid this part, so she decided to make the most of it. "I know this has been a difficult few days for you all. I've not been clear-headed or easy to get along with. All of you probably have had some idea in your heads of how I would be when I learned about the Parallel Society. Gram, most of all. Yet none of it turned out as any of you could have planned. I certainly didn't expect any of it."

Elliot chuckled. "You did perfectly fine."

"I don't know if this is a typical week for you guys, and I'm not sure I want to know. But I also realized that I've been fooling myself into thinking I can go back. I can't. When Darin broke in here and went into that book, it was over for him. Same for me. You can't unlearn what you've learned. And here's the thing I really have to admit — when we drove home, beaten and tired, I had a smile on my face. We had won, and that felt really good. Special." She stepped in front of the group. "I don't want to lose that feeling."

Sully put out his hand. "Does this mean you'll join us?"

"Yes." She took his hand. "If you'll have me."

Elliot and Gram stepped forward with arms out and hugs ready. "Happy to have you!" Elliot said.

Gram held her tight. "I've been so worried you'd leave

us."

"What?" Roni's throat tightened. She wanted to scream. "Why didn't you say so? Why did you keep pushing me away?"

"Because this is a commitment for the rest of your life. You had to make the choice to join us despite the bad. I'm glad you enjoyed the feeling of victory, but there are tough times in this business. A lot of them. We had to make sure you had the thickest skin possible for it."

Roni accepted the answer but did not believe it entirely. She had too much firsthand knowledge of Gram's tough side to buy that it was all an act for Roni's benefit.

"Well," Sully said, "now that's all settled, it's late and I'm tired. Good night." He walked off.

"I think I shall join him. Sleep sounds like a good idea." Elliot followed him away.

Gram held Roni at arm's length. "You're going to make me proud, right?"

"Of course," Roni said.

"Because we still don't know who hired Darin, and that troubles me. Things may not settle down anytime soon."

"Don't worry about me. I'll do my part."

"You've got a lot to learn, but I think you can handle it."

"I can't wait to get started."

Gram's face brightened. "Good. You saw the Special Library. Your first task is to organize and catalog that mess. Should only take a year or two. Maybe three. But that's the beauty of having a job for life. You've got time. So, you do like the boys and get some sleep. I've still got to hang the books we used for those small rips from the farmhouse. Then I'll sleep, too. Work starts at six tomorrow morning."

Roni forced a smile as they walked back to the elevator. She did not want to look too eager. After saying goodnight, she left the bookstore and headed to her apartment. The smile on her face became one of anticipation and determination.

What she said about the thrill in victory had been true, but it was not the reason for her decision to stay. It was the library. That special library held all the knowledge of the Society. That was the reason she joined the group. If answers were to be found anywhere, she would found them in those books — answers to all her lost time.

Her smile faded. She had to be ready for what that meant. She had to prepare.

Because she had a dark feeling that Gram knew the answers already.

RONI'S ADVENTURES CONTINUE IN

BOOK ON THE ISLE

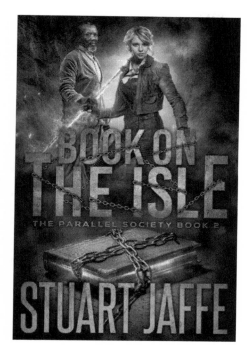

With a year in the Parallel Society under her belt, Veronica "Roni" Rider still feels like an outsider. Relegated to the basement library, she seeks some way to assert herself and find her place. Her chance arrives when she is sent on a mission into the Infinity Caverns to locate mystical stones in a lost universe. But the journey unearths many of the team's secrets, and the pressures upon them threaten to destroy their fragile group.

Then they discover the hellspiders and all bets are off.

**Don't miss out on Stuart Jaffe's bestselling series
The Max Porter Paranormal Mysteries!**

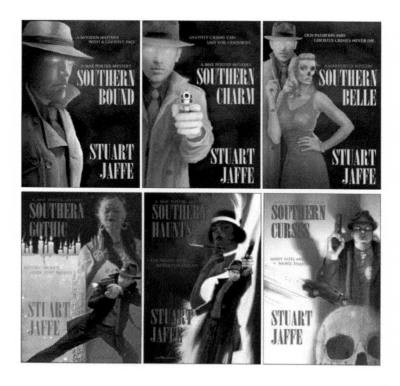

From ancient curses to witch covens, World War II secrets
to local lore, underground boxing to underground
chambers, Max Porter and his team investigate it all.

Don't miss a single story in the bestselling series,
the Max Porter Paranormal Mysteries.

ACKNOWLEDGMENTS

Starting a new series is always difficult. There's a significant amount of creation beyond the specific story that goes into everything - locations, magic systems, histories, monsters, etc. If done right, much of these things will continue to hold up for the entire series. So, I must give extra special thanks to all of those people who read advanced copies of this book and helped shape things. Whether from finding typos to helping me avoid infodumps, every comment from these people made a difference in the final story. Thank you to all of my Launch Team. Also, thanks to Deranged Doctor Design for lovely new covers. And no thank you section would be complete without thanking my beautiful bride and our lovely spawn. Thanks Glory and Gabe.

Finally, I want to thank you, my reader. I'm very excited about this new series, and I appreciated you taking a chance on it with me. Thank you.

ABOUT THE AUTHOR

Stuart Jaffe is the madman behind the *Nathan K* thrillers, *The Max Porter Paranormal Mysteries, The Malja Chronicles, The Bluesman, Founders, Real Magic,* and much more. He trained in martial arts for over a decade until a knee injury ended that practice. Now, he plays lead guitar in a local blues band, The Bootleggers, and enjoys life on a small farm in rural North Carolina. For those who continue to keep count, the animal list is as follows: one dog, two cats, three aquatic turtles, twenty-two chickens, and a horse. As best as he's been able to manage, Stuart has made sure that the chickens and the horse do not live in the house.

For more information about Stuart and his books, please visit *www.stuartjaffe.com*